Class B Angel

Kye-Keyann Bates
Copyright 2014

Chapter 1

"To a friend: I'm still counting down the days."

The words hung in the air as twenty-five teenagers sat motionless while I stood at the front of the classroom in front of the interactive whiteboard.

My name: Asanté Bulivard. I was seventeen years old, chocolate brown skin, jet black hair, bushy eyebrows and a potato-shaped nose. It was April 2012. I looked around at the eyes and faces of my fellow classmates. Shock and awe. No one had expected those words to come out of me as my first-liner. I knew what they must have been thinking: 'Asanté?' 'Who's the friend?' 'Counting down 'till what?' and the like. However, I knew when people wrote what was on their minds the written words could be surprising. I took my seat as another student arose to take my place. As I sat, I felt as if everyone were watching me, so I looked at the pink marble desk in which I sat and refused to look away from it until the next student spoke. The tension lifted, my legs stopped shaking and I could breathe again.

Later, at lunch, I sat at a round grey table which divided along the center. I looked at the mixed multitude sitting with me at the crowded table made to comfortably seat six, but now sat thirteen. There was an artsy girl with short red hair, Peyton, a smart, tall, skinny guy with curly black hair, Caleb, another guy with blonde hair, Alex, another girl with curly red hair, Christina, and a tall, skinny girl with curly brunette hair, Amanda, just to name a few of who I sat with. Some would see these students as faces, but I saw them as souls diverse in ethnicity and personality. I tried to reach out to them, being a Christian. I would ask them what good things had happened in their life over the past week, what good things they hoped would happen in the upcoming week, if something happened during the week which could not have been just luck, and the like, but of course as a Christian I had received opposition in times past, but there was Reagan I had to be an example for. She also sat at the table. We were of the same faith in Christianity, being Pentecostal and even went to the same church. I never had someone to hold as an example of how to reach out to my fellow peers at school, but now Reagan was there. Reagan was fifteen, had brown hair past her waist and never wore makeup or revealing clothing. I wanted her to feel God's presence more in the school, sense students' spiritual needs and reach out to them. Things I had just then, as a senior in high school, begun to do.

With her being new to the school, as well as being a sophomore, I felt she had more time to do in the school what I had not done: reach out to people. Granted, I spent a great deal of time picking on her and giving her a hard time simply because I was glad to finally not be the only Pentecostal in my school, but I also wanted to be an example of a good Christian in school to her. Of course, taking things from her bag and hiding them at times in random places might have been counterintuitive to my efforts, but overall we shared laughs and throughout the school year we had become friends.

After school we walked home just as any other day since we lived in the same neighborhood close by. We passed by a local bank along the way. I saw her reach into her pockets as if to search for something.

"Hey, I gotta use the ATM," she said and took off towards the bank doors.

"Alright," I said and followed.

It was not a big bank. The outside walls were blue, but the inside walls were grey. There were two glass doors to enter through which led to the grey tiled lobby. To the left was the teller area and to the right was the white ATM. I listened to the beeps as she pushed the buttons on the machine. I looked up at the camera on the ceiling, as I did in any building, and watched it rotate. In the reflection of its surrounding glass I saw a man stumble in wearing brown boots, blue jeans and a dark jacket with a hand in one of its pockets. I looked from the camera to him and something immediately felt wrong about him which made my muscles tighten. For an unknown reason I really wanted his jacket. There was nothing special about it. It was a simple black and brown jacket. Why did I want his jacket? The man staggered to the spot just under the camera, pulled his hand out of his pocket and pointed something at the camera above. With a loud bang the glass shattered into tiny pieces and a mixture of screams and gasps soon followed. Reagan's shriek, for whatever reason, caught the man's attention. The man pulled back his greasy ponytail and walked towards her. I felt something else wrong as well, but I could only focus on the man with the gun. I instinctively stepped between him and her. Only when he was inches from me did I begin to think to grab his gun, but by then it was too late. His gun was pointed at me. I could feel the steel through my hoodie as he put the barrel to my stomach. I froze in terror as he stood there, scruffy-bearded and yellow-eyed.

His breath reeked of alcohol as he said, "move."

When I did not move, his gun moved from my stomach to my chest. I reached behind me and grabbed Reagan's arm. She was cold with fear and I could sense it almost. I stepped sideways, taking her with me, but was stopped short when his gun again touched my chest.

"Uh-uh," he said, "the girl stays with me."

My fear began to be replaced with anger as he grinned and flashed his yellow teeth.

"Remove," my voiced cracked so I spoke again trying to sound more confident, "move your gun away from me and I'll let her go."

Instantly her free arm grabbed mine and she squeezed. I had no intention of giving her to this monster, but I needed to get the gun off of me if I was going to be able to get us out of there alive.

"Alright," he said and lowered his gun.

I took this as an opportunity to kick him in the groin and quickly reach for his gun, hoping the pain would cause him to release his weapon. Adrenaline began to rush through me the moment before I kicked, after which my mind was focused only on getting his gun, not noticing my kick had no immediate effect. Having never been drunk, I did not think drunkenness to be a painkiller. With his free hand he ripped my hand off of his gun, put his gun in my side and fired.

It all happened so fast. The burning in my body. Reagan cried and screamed at the other customers and employees to help, but no one moved. I fell to the floor, bleeding, as he pulled her by her hair. And no one did a single thing.

I passed out.

'Wake up, Asanté. Wake up.'

A soft, gentle, soothing female voice echoed in my head. When I opened my eyes I was surrounded by white and sky blue. I sat up and at first thought I was hallucinating, but one touch of the white substance confirmed my sight. Clouds. I was laying in a bed, no, a sea of clouds.

"I must be dead," I heard myself say.

"No, you're not dead," came a voice from what looked like a cloud clump the size of a door.

I was shocked and fell silent. A man walked through the cloud clump in front of me with a clipboard and pen in hand. He wore only a white robe and had dark brown hair. Standing in front of me, he looked me over.

"Where am I?" I asked.

"First," he said, "my name is David and you're in the 'Awakening' which is a room in-side of what used to be called Abraham's Bo-som."

He looked at me with a raised eyebrow. I recognized the name.

"The heaven before heaven, right?" I asked.

He continued, "there has been major remodifications from its original design, but come along now. You're awake."

I was about to stand up until I looked down. I was sitting on a cloud shaped like a bed and the ground below was also made up of clouds.

"If you're worried about falling," said David, "don't. Have faith."

"Like Peter?" I asked while putting a foot down.

He turned around and walked back through the cloud clump he had emerged from earlier. I stood up and the clouds felt cushiony beneath my feet. David's head appeared out of the cloud.

"Before you continue on," he said, "you'll have to take your shoes and socks off and leave them behind. Holy ground and all."

I took my shoes and socks off and the clouds felt warm and soft on my feet rather than cold and wet. I walked towards the cloud clump and tried to resist the urge to hold my breath and instead have faith and breathe. I still ended up holding my breath briefly.

Going through the cloud brought me into another giant sea of clouds, but this place had mountains and hills of clouds and was full of people. Everywhere I looked, humans (or were the ones with wings angels) were walking, talking, running and, no, I had to just be seeing things. Flying! People were actually flying! There was no way I could really be seeing this, but there it was. People were actually flying with and without wings. David tapped me on the shoulder, waking me from my daze.

"This is the central plane," he said, "and the entire area is the Class B Angel Headquarters, or CBAHQ as you may soon call it. Now follow me."

David led me through the seemingly chaotic hustle and bustle of people walking and running about. As we got closer to the hills and mountains of clouds I saw people walking into them instead of over them and disappeared. How did people not get lost here? I was so busy looking around I did not see David take a turn and ended up walking through a cloud. What appeared before me was the only non cloud room I had seen since I woke up. It had light grey stone walls with pillars of light blue. Falling around the pillars were two purple ribbons in a downward spiral, but the ribbons were not touching the pillars. The pillars lined a walkway to a circular table on the far end of the room where I saw the silhouettes of people sitting and talking behind a thick purple curtain.

"The boy is dangerous," came a deep male voice.

I stood still and listened.

"Smart," continued the voice, "but dangerous. We should-"

"Kill him now!" shouted a high pitch male voice which was followed by hysterical laughter from the same voice.

"Must you always interrupt people?" asked a female voice, "we can always get the best out of him before we-"

Something grabbed my shoulder and pulled me back into the central plane. I turned around to see David with a serious look on his face.

"Don't get lost," he said.

What a thing to say when there is nothing except clouds to use as land markers. Who were those people? What were they talking about? Oh well. I had to continue on. I followed David closely this time and this time he looked over his shoulder more often. Finally we arrived at a mountain cloud.

"Enter through here," he said.

"What's inside?" I asked.

He crossed his arms and said, "you'll see."

So I looked at the mountain cloud in front of me and walked through. What I saw on the other side was another sea of clouds, but there was a drawer with four compartments as well. The top compartment was labeled 'underwear,' the next 'boxer briefs,' then 'boxers' and lastly 'custom.' On top of the drawer was a plaque which read, "Finally, my brethren, be strong in the Lord, and in the power of his might. Put on the whole armour of God, that ye may be able to stand against the wiles of the devil. For we wrestle not against flesh and blood, but against principalities, against powers, against the rulers of the darkness of this world, against spiritual wickedness in high places. Wherefore take unto you the whole armour of God, that ye may be able to withstand in the evil day, and having done all, to stand. Stand therefore, having your loins girt about with truth, and having on the breastplate of righteousness; And your feet shod with the preparation of the gospel of peace; Above all, taking the shield of faith, wherewith ye shall be able to quench all the fiery darts of the wicked. And take the helmet of salvation, and the sword of the Spirit, which is the word of God: (Ephesians 6:10-17 KJV English)."

After a moment's thought, I connected the dots. I was putting on the armor of God. So I opened the boxers compartment and took out a blue pair. Once I closed the drawer, the labels changed. The top now read 'B.C.', the next, 'Medieval,' followed by 'Modern' and then 'Custom.' I looked through the medieval breast plates, but they seemed heavy, so I looked through the modern ones and found front halves of bullet-proof vests. I was confused at first, but there was no one to ask questions to so I took the black half-vest. Next to choose from was shoes. I chose to open the custom compartment first this time. Inside was a note which read, "Imagine." What was I supposed to imagine? I turned around to go back to the central plane and ask David for help, but the cloud pile was gone. Eventually I figured I had to imagine some shoes, so I imagined a pair of high-top sneakers with big cushions on the insides with gel padding for the soles. The outside was black and had no laces, but had holes for them. There was a bright blue x on the front face of the shoe as well as the heel. The bottom of the shoe had an engraved x.

Within seconds I watched the pair of shoes I imagined form from thin air in front of me. I set the shoes down with the boxers and half-vest. The next to choose from was shields. I did not bother looking at other compartments. I wanted my own custom shield. I imagined a large, curved triangular shield with a gold margin. The inside was a bright red with bright blue fire in the middle. Inside the fire was a black x. I imagined the shield to be worn on my back. For the helmet I imagined a long black cloak with a hood which blocked light from reflecting off of my face so no one could see it. There was a big white x across where my chest would be. The bottom of the cloak went to where my high-tops would end and from the hips down it formed an upside down funnel which split at the middle of the front, with the width of the split increasing the further down it went.

Finally, it was time for a sword. I had played many video-games before and had seen almost everything about a galaxy far, far away so I already knew what kind of sword I wanted. I imagined a laser sword hilt. The sword itself was a nine feet long katana made of black water and black light. At the end of the katana extruded a two feet by two feet white x to the side which gave the weapon a key shape. At least, it was how I imagined it. The sword formed on top of the shelf in front of the plaque, but it was not as long as I had imagined and was instead a double-edged sword rather than a katana, which confused me. It seemed to be barely longer than three feet, maybe forty inches including the eight inch handle. The x was probably seven or eight inches diagonally. I took the sword in my hand and the shelf fell through the clouds. I looked around for another cloud pile, but there was none. I figured the next thing I had to do was to put on the armor of God. I pressed the blue button on the hilt and the sword disappeared.

"Um, okay," I said.

I picked up the blue boxers from the bottom of the pile of clothes and immediately the clothes I already had on ripped off and flew away.

"Whoa! Dude!" I said, as if anyone was there to hear.

I felt something ride up my legs and looked down to see the blue boxers. Next the half-vest attached itself to my chest, followed by the shoes slipping onto my feet. The shield attached to my back and sides and fused with the vest. The cloak floated in front of me. I stood there waiting, expecting it to come to me, but it just remained floating. I decided to try and put it on myself which resumed the process. My shoes were surprisingly comfortable without socks, but my coat only covered my arms and torso, leaving my bare legs to be revealed and there were no pants around.

"If you need pants," said David behind me which startled me and made me jump, "I have a pair here."

I turned around to see him holding a pair of black pants which seemed to be pajama pants draped across his arm. In his other hand he still held his clipboard and pen with which he began to write as I continued to dress myself.

"Interesting choice of armor," he said, "do you play a lot of video games or watch a lot of cartoons?"

"It builds creativity," I answered him.

The pants were thick like cotton, but felt like silk on my legs. Pockets lined the sides of my legs in addition to front and back pockets. Each pocket had a zipper hidden under the material, making the pockets nigh invisible from the outside.

"It seems that you've already had an idea of your dream character in mind," said David, "but have you included wings?"

"I get wings, too!?" I asked.

Before David could answer I imagined having two large wings protruding from my back, the left wing being black and the right white, with a smaller, narrower wing below each being the same color as the larger wing above.

The wings appeared on my back and David wrote on his clipboard. I did not feel a pull on my back at all from the added weight of the wings. It was almost as if they were not there at all, but with a little concentration and effort I quickly learned to flap and fold them.

"Well," he began, "that takes care of that. As I'm sure you noticed, not everyone here has wings. Wings are given as a sign of ranking, not a necessary means of flight, to certain Class B Angels."

"What are Class B Angels?" I asked.

He waved his hand and said, "you'll learn about that soon enough. Is there a reason you don't want people seeing your face?"

The main reason was because of the nervousness I got when everyone was looking at me, but there was also the coolness factor of it all.

"It looks cool," I said, "adds mystery."

He pointed his pen at my hands and said, "you do realize that people can still see your hands, correct?"

I had not thought about my hands.

"Do you got a pair of gloves with you? Preferably black?" I asked.

David sighed, reached behind him and brought forth a thin pair of what appeared to be black leather gloves, but something about them seemed special.

"Before I give you these," he said, "you must tell me why you are trying to hide your identity."

I looked him in the eye and said, "well to start I don't know anyone here, but from the looks of it there's people here from all over the world. That being said, anybody could be anybody. This ain't heaven, so I don't want someone to hate me here and then find out who I was on Earth and torture my family or something like that. Also, I want to be seen as dark and mysterious."

I assume he wrote all of what I said on his clipboard as I spoke. He handed me the gloves.

"Well," he said, "you definitely won't have a problem with that in your getup."

The gloves were very comfortable, but I could not feel them on my fingertips. I folded a wing in front of me and touched it. To my surprise I could actually feel the feathers as if I were touching them barehanded. I also noticed on the backhand side of the gloves were a white x. How could I have missed a glowing white x when I first put them on?

"What kind of gloves are these?" I asked.

David shrugged his shoulders. "I don't know," he said, "I was given them anonymously by someone to give to you. Same with the pants."

Someone knew I would need pants and want gloves?

"Anyway," he continued, "time to move on."

Behind him was a cloud clump and we walked through it into the central plane.

'Wow, you look different,' echoed a soft gentle voice, 'but different in a good way. Mysterious.'

It was the same voice I had heard in the Awakening.

I tapped him on the shoulder, "David?"

He looked down from his clipboard at me, "yes?"

'Oh please don't reveal me,' the voice quickly echoed, 'not yet at least.'

I decided then to keep this voice a mystery for myself for now and avoid claims of schizophrenia.

"What..." I had to think of something else, but could not. "Never mind," I finally said.

He raised an eyebrow and said, "follow me."

I forgot the previous experience of not keeping my eyes on David while following him and I watched the people of the central plane fly around for one second. One second became two. Two seconds became three and before I knew it something white passed over me and the sky was clear again. I looked around and saw another empty sea of clouds.

"Is every room infinite clouds? Oh wait! David!"

I turned around and ran through the cloud clump. Back in the central plane, I looked around for David, but he was nowhere within view.

"Dang it," I mumbled.

I flapped my wings to fly, but I stayed on the ground.

"You must have just awoken," came a voice to my right.

I looked to see a peach skinned boy, about my height, with white spiky hair, sky-blue eyes and two large white feathered wings which, like mine, could encase him. He wore a white cloak and tan sandals.

"Yeah," I said.

"You need to release your mind from the physical," he continued.

He had to be sixteen at the most.

"Thanks," I said, "I'm-"

"Don't tell me your name just yet," he said while raising his hand, "I think we were in the Awakening together. And since you're here rather than with David, I'm guessing you lost him before you learned about being a Class B Angel."

"We were in the awakening together? I didn't see you."

"We appeared there at the same time, but I woke up first and asked questions and I've learned quite a lot about this place and how things work."

"Oh okay cool. So then what's going on here? What is all this? How do I fly? Why was I given wings? Are you the one who gave the pants and gloves to David to give to me?"

"Let's start with flying first. The rest will come in time. As for the gloves and pants, no. I didn't give you those. But I can give you flight lessons. Forget your wings and instead imagine yourself flying, because you already are. That's how you first get off the clouds. To go somewhere you put your weight into it. You don't necessarily have to lean too far, but a simple nudge in that direction will do the trick. To fly faster, focus on flying faster. The same concept applies to slowing down."

"Oh. Thank you," I said.

He was right. I was standing on clouds, so I was already flying. I closed my eyes, kept my wings folded in and imagined myself flying just a little higher. A few seconds later I felt a tap on my head. I opened my eyes to see the boy.

"Don't fly too high," he said, "it's easy to get lost in infinity."

I looked down. The people below us looked like ants.

"Follow me," he said.

He arched his wings, backflipped and dove down toward the sea of clouds below. I slowly leaned forward and down. It was as if I was at the top of a roller-coaster and was just beginning to descend from the first drop. Roller-coasters made me very nervous. It was not the twists or turns, but the drops I was not fond of. The thought of being strapped down to something plummeting to the ground was not appealing to me; nor the inability to breathe while dropping and my stomach wanting to jump out of my mouth. Flying felt very different. I controlled every aspect of my descent and the gentle breeze on my face felt pleasant.

'You look great for your first time flying,' echoed the soft voice, 'don't lose your friend.'

My friend? Oh! The boy! I was closer to the people now and scanned the cloudy sea for any sign of him and managed to catch a glimpse of him as he turned behind a cloud hill. I focused on flying faster and in time I caught up to him, but it did take some dodging and weaving through people.

Shortly after, he descended in front of a cloud clump and stood. I descended next to him, but remained afloat.

"Where are we? I asked, "and how do you not get lost here?"

He shrugged his shoulders. "I still don't know how to navigate this place completely," he answered, "David brought me here and I remembered how to get back, but I think each

doorway or cloud portal has a certain distin-
guishable shape or characteristic beyond the
doorways that are our size, the ones shaped
like hills and the ones shaped like mountains.
Anyway, once you awoke we were supposed to
start our training by going here first, but I've already been in here so there's nothing new to
me just yet."

"Oh, okay," I said and followed him
through the cloud portal.

On the other side was a large room with
cloud floors and cloud walls, but no ceiling. The
room had a downward slope from where I was
hovering and desks lined along the slope as if
the room was a classroom. At the bottom of the
slope was a black podium facing the desks and
a large chalkboard behind it. The boy and I
each sat at a desk and a man appeared from
behind the chalkboard. He wore a blue robe
and had short brown curly hair. He walked to
the podium and scratched his head.

"Could you sit a little closer?" he asked
the class of two. I flew out of my seat and
moved two rows ahead.

"Now," he began, "my name is Professor."

"Professor?" I asked.

"Yes?" he responded, "what's your
question?" He smiled at the joke. "Now," he
continued, "Vete has gone through this initial
orientation before."

"Vete?" I asked.

"It's the name I chose," said Vete.

"You chose your name?" I asked Vete.

"Yes," answered Professor, "and now you will choose your name, Asanté."

"How do you know my name?" I asked him.

"We'll be getting to that later," answered Professor, "but for now it's time to choose your new name. Your Class B Angel name. Just keep in mind that it cannot be changed and it is how you'll most always be referred to."

"Yes, sir," I said.

I began to think of many names, but Vete's name stuck out to me. I began to feel the pressure of everyone, all two of them, watching me, but inside my armor, my cloak and hood, I felt safe and hidden. I slowly rose from my desk and walked to the chalkboard. Professor gave me a piece of yellow chalk to write with.

"Thank you," I said.

I had watched many different anime shows and played many video-games, so unique names were not foreign to me, but how could I top a name like Vete? What did his name even mean? On the board I wrote the letters T-E-K-O-N.

"Teckon?" asked Professor with an emphasis on the first vowel.

"No, sir," I said, "Tek, on. Emphasis on the 'on.' Tekon."

It took me a while to read my new name without emphasizing the first vowel as well. Then I remembered a video game which was spelled very similar to my new name. Dang it, I thought, I just changed one letter from a game and moved the emphasis.

"Tekon," said Vete.

I looked at him.

"Nice name," he said.

"Thanks," I said.

I gave the chalk back to Professor and sat down at my desk beside Vete.

"Well, Tekon," said Professor, "first thing's first. How did you get here?"

A very good question. The last thing I remembered was …

"I died," I said.

"No, you didn't die."

"Sir?"

"How did you die? Don't answer out loud. Just think about it. Now, here's a fact: you're not dead. You're here because something on Earth happened that would've killed you because of your selfless act of putting your life in danger to save and protect someone else's from someone possessed by what you humans call a demon. Under normal circumstances you would be dead. However you have been chosen, before your birth, to be recruited as a Class B Angel," he began writing the term on the board, "should you ever fall into that type of situation. Your name has been on the list long before you were born. Now that's all stage one."

He began to write on the board again.

"Stage two was choosing your appearance and name, which you've already done. Stage three is your training. After that, you are officially considered to be a Class B Angel."

'Stage 1,' 'Stage 2' and 'Stage 3' were written on the board under 'Class B Angel.'

"Now, after stage three you are free to quit if you so choose, however only one person has ever quit. Now, the purpose of a Class B Angel, or CBA, is to watch over humans and fight against spiritual principalities, against powers, rulers of darkness and spiritual wickedness in high places."

He wrote 'Ephesians 6:10-17 KJV English' on the board.

"These are the core verses of a Class B Angel. Remember them. Know them. Live them. The reason why Class B Angels even exist is because God is calling back the angels in droves and we need replacements. No one knows why God is calling us back, but He is and has left the details to the Cherubim Information Center, or CIC, which orchestrates everything CBA related. Now, as chosens you will each be given a book at some point in your training that explains things in more detail and contains information only for chosens to know. And that concludes the initial orientation. Any questions, Tekon?"

I had a lot of information to take in. I was chosen before I was born? God was calling back the angels? I had to replace a guardian angel?

"No, sir," was all I could say.

Professor began to erase the writing on the chalkboard. "Then you may go to the training room," said Professor, "It'll be the mountain size portal directly in front of you when you leave the classroom."

"Yes, sir," I said, "thank you."

Vete and I left the classroom and entered the central plane and, just like Professor said, there was a mountain size cloud portal ahead of us.

"One would think the size of the portal relates to the size of the room," I said as we flew, "but most of the small portals lead to an infinite room, except for one room I saw with no clouds at all. So where do the big portals lead to? A finite room?"

Vete looked at me and asked, "You've been in a room without clouds?"

"Yeah," I said, wondering if I should tell him what I heard.

We arrived at the mountain cloud and I walked through before he could ask me anything else.

Chapter 2

Inside, the room was huge. There was no cloud flooring, but instead a massive rainforest surrounded me.

"Was it like this?" Vete asked behind me.

"No," I said as I looked around.

A nearby bush rustled and a large man emerged from it with a group of five people behind him. He was wearing a camouflage jumpsuit with camouflage boots and a camouflage hat. Out of the five people behind him, three were girls and two were boys. The first guy, who was slightly muscular, wore a biker helmet, black leather pants, a spiked metal breast plate and carried a large, round, wooden shield. The other boy was short and scrawny. He had blonde hair, blue eyes and wore glasses, a metal spiked helmet, a front half of a bulletproof vest, blue jeans and a digital watch. The three girls each had brunette hair which went to their mid back, hazel eyes and wore a bright blue tiara, a bright sleeveless pink dress with a white unbuttoned sweater jacket over it, a pair of bright blue sandals and a pink flower in their hair. The man in camouflage looked us over.

"Well howdy, my name's Hunter. You must be Vete and Tekon," he said as he firmly shook our hands. His brown eyes tried to pierce through the darkness of my hood and he asked, "there a reason you don't want nobody seein' yer face?" Before I could answer he moved on and said, "So we got an anime fan and a Jedi fan. At least y'all got a theme goin' unlike those two fellas. And looky here, we got chosens in our midst! I got a special book for y'all later. Alright now meetcher crew. Y'all'll be trainin' together."

He walked away and disappeared into the forest. The man with the biker helmet was Larry (he decided to keep his Earth name), was twenty-two years old and had red hair and green eyes. The younger boy, thirteen, named himself Terminator and showed me how his watch could produce a green circular laser shield with the press of a button. The three girls refused to talk. Larry said they had not said a word since they awoke.

'I hope your training goes well,' echoed the soft, gentle voice in my head.

Hunter came back to the group and explained some of the meaning of our armor and told us the usage of each would be tested in each section of the training room. The forest would test our "girdles of truth" (I called them "truth boxers"). The city would test our breast-plates of righteousness. The desert would test our "footwear of peace." The sea would test our helmets of salvation. The mountains, which actually had three parts, would first test our shields of faith, then our swords of the spirit and finally the combination of all of our armor.

We followed Hunter to a giant tree in the middle of the forest.

"Now," he said, eyeing us, "let's learn y'all how ta fly."

The girls' eyes lit up and big grins grew on their faces. Terminator adjusted his glasses.

"Now I know I'm dreaming," said Larry.

"When yer flyin' you don't need no wings like Vete and Tekon here," began Hunter, "All you need to do is..." the rest he said in unison with Vete, "release your mind from the physical."

Hunter and the trainees looked at Vete.

"Tekon and I are gonna go explore," said Vete as he rose to the air.

I rose after him.

"Whoa yo, how'd you do that, yo!?" asked Terminator.

"Alright," said Hunter, "but stay in the forest and come back once they've learned to fly, ya hear?"

"Yes, sir," I answered him, and then to Terminator, "Hunter will teach you."

As Vete and I flew off, I looked back to see Terminator jumping and flapping his arms. Vete and I flew above the forest trees and could finally see the clear blue sky. At some point he stopped in the air and stood as if the air beneath his feet was solid ground.

"So," said Vete, "tell me what you saw."

"What?" I asked.

He crossed his arms and said, "In the first room you saw with no clouds."

In our conversation Vete had asked me question after question about things I had seen, how much I knew and what my thoughts were about everything. I did mention the soft voice in my head. He did not ask about my armor, but he did ask about the conditions upon my arrival to the spiritual world, or the CBA world.

"That's not important," I said.

"That's fine," he replied.

Then it was my turn to ask questions. What I learned about him was, like me, he liked to explore new places. He would ask questions when presented with something he knew little or nothing about and he had a very high IQ as well. I did not ask him any personal questions about his past life and neither did he to me aside from asking how I arrived. The leafs rustled below and Terminator emerged. He shakily flew up right in front of us, but faced away from us. He bobbed up and down as he began to cup his hands to his eyes to look for us. When Vete and I finally came into view he jumped, flew back suddenly and just barely caught his glasses.

"Took ya long enough," I said.

"Yo I just started flying," said Terminator as he adjusted his glasses, "give me a break, yo."

We laughed, but Vete did not. "Let's go," said Vete.

I thought, at most, I was decent at flying, but looking over my shoulder as we flew made me feel I was more than decent. Terminator could not fly in a straight line and had a hard time controlling just how far left he banked or how fast his descents were. At one point he leaned too far and was flying backwards upside-down. I thought it was pretty cool until he slammed into a tree. Terminator of the Jungle. Vete flew with grace and ease. The systematic flapping of his majestic wings was flawless. He navigated the forest and weaved through tree trunks and branches with excellent precision. I, on the other hand, had to remember to keep my wings in a steady beat and skimmed a few branches. I actually flew through a branch when I first looked over my shoulder to see if Terminator was keeping up. When we got back to Hunter and the group, the girls were flying in a circle, giggling. Larry was sitting on a large portion of an uncovered root.

"Well if it ain't Tekon and Vete," said Hunter, "the dark phantom and the light angel."

Vete landed in front of Hunter. "Before we begin training," said Vete, "I have a question."

Surprise, surprise.

"Yeah?" responded Hunter.

"Our shield of faith is only as strong as our-"

"Bullseye!"

"So our-"

"Yup. Let's get started now. Gather 'round, y'all and let's pray."

Everyone held hands in a circle with Hunter except for one. I looked at Larry sitting on the root looking down and holding his wooden shield.

"Atheist," said Vete to me.

What?

"Atheist? Here?" I blurted out a bit too loud.

"Yes I'm an atheist," said Larry, "and to me this is all a big crazy dream. Very vivd, I might add. What? Let me guess. This is the part of the dream where you try to convert me right?"

If Atheists were here, then were people of other religions here as well? Muslims? Buddhists? Thousands of different denominations of Christianity?

"Are we allowed to do that here?" I asked no one.

"I would assume so," answered Vete, "this isn't heaven after all."

I felt a tug on my hand. It was Terminator. I instantly let go of his hand upon the realization of he and I being the only ones still holding hands.

"Now Larry we done talked 'bout this here already," I heard Hunter say.

31

Larry stood and said "I'm not doing it! None of this is real!"

I walked over to him and asked why he thought this was all just a dream, though I was beginning to wonder the same thing myself.

"One," said Larry as he held up a finger, "I was flying. Two," a second finger, "God isn't real. And three," a third finger, "if God is real then I wouldn't be here and He's the biggest jerk to ever exist!"

Terminator spoke up, "yo well think about it this way: if we pray we'll close our eyes and when you open them again you'll wake up, yo."

Terminator's words seemed to work. Hunter started the prayer once everyone had their heads bowed and eyes closed.

"Dear God our heavenly Father …" he began, but his voice slowly morphed into my mother's. It was a slow fade, a bit fuzzy at first, but the clarity surely came and I heard my mother praying. I opened my eyes. I was no longer in the forest surrounded by greenery in a circle of seven other people. I was laying in a hospital bed. My mother, light-skinned with short hair which did not grow, was praying over me with one hand in mine. Connected to my other hand was a larger, darker man. My step-dad. Both had their heads bowed and eyes closed.

"What?" I asked.

Both of their eyes opened and my mom bursted into tears, though her face told me she had been crying a lot already. She began to thank God and I went back to sleep. When I next awoke, I was alone in the room. There was a TV mounted up on the wall directly across from me. I looked around for the remote control.

"How ya feeling?"

I was not alone. My step-dad sat to the far left wall with a tablet in hand.

"Sir?" I asked.

"How ya feeling?" he responded.

"Fine-how-'bout-you?"

The words came out of my mouth like clockwork, courtesy of my mother making me read a book about fifty-five essential etiquette rules five times. One rule was when people asked how I was, I was to answer them and then ask them the same, thus showing I was as interested in them as they were in me.

My step-dad smiled and asked, "Hungry?"

My stomach wasted no time in answering with a low growl.

"Yes, sir," I answered.

The hospital food was not the best, but it was good enough. There was a cup of water, a cup of yogurt, a ham sandwich, mashed potatoes and collard greens. My step-dad handed me a small bottle of hot sauce and a soda which my mother had snuck in for me. Near the end of my meal my mother walked in. She wore a long jean skirt and a red top with flower designs.

"Hey," she said as she waved.

She pulled up a chair to my bed and sat down beside me. All of the questions came. How did I feel? What did I remember? What did the guy look like? What did I do? Did I see which direction the man took Reagan through any windows? Reagan and I were in everyone's prayers. It was not my fault. I stopped paying attention after Reagan was mentioned. Reagan. I had failed to protect her from a drunken man who could have done any number of things to her while I was laid up in the hospital. No one knew where she was or if she was even alive. Why? Because I could not protect her; I could not save her. I fought back the tears which tried to escape as my mother talked. There was one voice I had not yet heard from which I had expected to be one of the first voices to hear.

"Where's Myla?" I asked.

My little sister, Myla, was light-skinned like my mother, loud, curious and energetic. My mother told me she was in the waiting room with some of our church family. The door opened again and a male doctor in a white coat walked in. In his hand was a clear bag with a small metal object inside.

"You're quite the miracle, young man," said the doctor.

He sounded exactly like David.

"Yes he is," said my mother.

"This bullet should have killed you," said the doctor, "it went between the bones of your rib cage, through the top of your stomach and lodged inside the bottom of your heart, but by the grace or will of God, you're still alive."

"We're a praying family," said my mother.

The doctor then went on to explain how it was even a miracle the bullet was found and the emergency treatment I received. I was to stay in bed and rest a few days, then go home and rest some more. Schoolwork would be brought to me here so I would not fall too far behind. I was two days behind already. After the doctor left, there was the police questioning to go through. Two officers, one a blonde male with brown eyes and the other a caramel skinned female with her hair in a ponytail, came to question me alone about everything. It was practically as if my mother were asking me questions again. After the last questions were answered, the room grew darker. I thought there was a problem with the lighting, but the way the room darkened was too unnatural to be electronic failure.

"Quit now, or you'll never see your friend again," said the male.

I looked at him and for an unknown reason I wanted his badge and his gun. It took me a while to register what he said.

"Sir?" I asked.

"Oo they're so cute when they first awake," said the female.

She leaned over the railing at the end of my bed and I felt a sudden attraction to her along with a pressure on my chest from an unknown source.

"What?" I managed to ask.

"I wonder what his other body looks like," she said as she looked me over.

I was beginning to wonder what her body looked like under the uniform, but I looked into her eyes to avoid looking elsewhere and she smiled. My head began to ache, my heart raced and my feet began to tingle. The pressure was increasing and I felt trapped. My eyes slowly moved from her eyes to her nose, then mouth, then neck. I darted my gaze towards the male.

"What's the matter dearie?" asked the woman.

My eyes met hers again like a puppy yanked by its leash and the struggle started over, but my eyes could not meet her gaze for long before falling south again. My chest and head hurt immensely and I could not form words in my mouth, but in my mind I screamed for Jesus. The male officer grabbed the woman's arm.

"That's enough," he said.

"Ooooh," whined the woman. She stood up straight and the pressure on my chest released. "We'll have fun some other time," she said with a wink.

My head stopped throbbing. Able to speak again, I asked what was going on.

"Tell anyone of what just happened and you'll never see Reagan again," said the man.

"You know where she is? Where is she!?" I asked.

The woman put her finger to her lips. "Shhh. It's our little secret," she said and winked at me again.

The two officers left the room and I was temporarily alone with my thoughts. What just happened? What was the pressure on my chest and head? Why did my feet begin to tingle? Why was I so attracted to the woman all of a sudden? Why did I want the man's badge and gun? Why did the room darken? They knew about Reagan and where she was. Something was not right there, but there was nothing I could do in the hospital. In the morning I would check myself out and begin my search for Reagan. For the next few hours various people from church came to say hi and drop off gifts. I paid just enough attention to be respectful and polite, but my mind was on the event which just occurred. One visitor did manage to break me from my thoughts. There was a knock on the door as normal, but a girl with hazel eyes and long brown hair peeked her head inside. Anna. She was another girl from church.

"Hey," she said softly.

"Hey!" exclaimed my mother.

She rose from her seat and embraced Anna as she walked in. Anna wore a grey long sleeve low cut shirt with a white tee-shirt under it, a jean skirt and black cloth shoes. She carried with her a medium sized brown purse from which she pulled out a bag of teriyaki flavored beef jerky.

"Thank you," I said, "you don't have to set that with the other stuff. I'll eat that one right now."

She handed me the food and we exchanged a smile. She and my mother talked for a while. I mostly listened, but when I could intervene I would say something here or there and make a joke to which she would laugh. Visiting hours ended too soon, I felt, and she had to leave. She walked out of the door and quietly said bye. I said bye back, thanked her for coming, we both smiled and she was gone.

The moment her presence left the room I was instantly engrossed in thoughts of the two officers. I tried to wrap my mind around what had happened, but I could not think straight and thoughts of Anna kept creeping into my mind. I tried to sleep, hours later, but I could not. I was too excited about what was happening. However, the excitement soon faded when my thoughts fell on Reagan. It was the last night I would be in the hospital. It mattered not whatever operation my body just underwent to get the bullet out. I had a friend to find. I had even more motivation to leave the hospital the next day after my parents told me Reagan's parents were going to pay me a visit. I could not let the visit happen. I could not face them. Originally, Reagan was not allowed to walk home after school, though she wanted to. Once her parents found out we went to the same high school and I also walked home from school they allowed her to walk with me. They trusted me to keep her safe from predators, but I failed them. They must have hated me. I lost their daughter. Their only child. I might as well have killed her myself - it would have made no difference. To get my mind off of the depression I drowned myself in TV. Commercials were great sleep inducers. There was an odd commercial I saw right before I drifted off. There was a clip of a pastor preaching. He was dark skinned, bald and round. I recognized him to be bishop D.T. Hakes. His voice was low, but airy.

He said, "let's begin this sermon with a prayer. Dear God our heavenly Father..."

When next I opened my eyes I was back in the forest, surrounded by greenery and seven other faces, six of which whose expressions alone told me I was not the only one to take a trip back to the land of the living. The six students were all wide-eyed. We casually released each other's hands.

'How was your first Prayer Life?' The soft gentle voice echoed in my head.

"What y'all here just experienced was a Prayer Life," said Hunter.

He reached over his shoulder and grabbed what appeared to be a camouflage rifle strapped to his back, but when he held it out in front of him I could see it was actually a long sword painted in camouflage with a gun handle, scope and trigger instead of a hilt. I recognized it to be a gunblade, but saw no hole for any bullets.

"When one of us angels is in physical contact with one o' y'all and prays," continued Hunter, "y'all'll return to your Earthly bodies. Once you pass training and become full fledged Class B Angels, y'all'll be able to have prayer lives on yer own."

"What happens to our bodies on Earth while we're here?" asked Vete, "do our bodies on Earth act and respond the way we would to any given situation? Do our bodies grow and mature based on those given situations just the same as we would had we not had our consciousness transported here? Do we grow and mature here as our bodies do? Do our bodies grow and mature there as we do here? Do we lose the time we spend here or do we regain our body's memories upon return? What happens to our bodies here when our consciousness returns to Earth?" Vete spit out the questions one right after the other with no time for response.

"Yo I couldn't catch all that, yo" said Terminator.

"Basically," I began to explain, "he's asking if our bodies and minds here are in sync with our bodies and minds in Earth."

"Oh," replied Terminator.

Hunter propped his gunblade on his shoulder and said "yes to everythang. Yer bodies are all on auto-pilot until your present consciousness returns. Once yer able to do a Prayer Life on yer own you'll keep yer mem'ries. Larry."

The sound of his name woke him from his daze. "Yeah?" he sheepishly asked.

"You still thankin' this a dream?" asked Hunter.

"Oh yeah," said Larry, "One hundred percent sure. I just woke up a while ago and now I'm back asleep."

Hunter smiled and the girls gasped. Terminator took his glasses off, wiped them on his pants and put them back on.

"Dude," was all I could say.

"What?" asked Larry.

"Stand, therefore, having your loins girt about with truth," said Vete.

"Huh?" asked Larry.

"The forest tests your honesty," Vete began to explain, "which here is manifested physically in the clothes you wear, specifically

41

your girdle, or in this case your underwear, which is something most people do not want exposed in public, but when you lie, the truth is exposed."

It was true. His outer layer of clothing quickly became transparent, revealing his white underwear and red hairy legs. The transparency of his helmet also revealed his curly red hair and beady green eyes.

Larry looked at himself and said, "hey! What's going on with my clothes!?"

"And when you don't have yer armor," said Hunter.

He then lunged at Larry, his sword stopping inches from Larry's transparent breastplate before Larry could even think to raise his shield.

"Yer wide open like a barn door in a hurricane," said Hunter as he poked Larry with his gunblade. The weapon went through the transparent armor. "The more you lie, the more people see straight through you. Not just physically, mind you."

"Your layers will return if you tell the truth," said Vete.

"Bullseye," said Hunter.

"I'm not lying!" said Larry, "I know this is just a dream!"

His armor and underwear completely vanished. The girls gasped again and placed their hands in front of each other's eyes.

"Yo, I don't need to see this, yo," said Terminator who took off his glasses.

"Whoa dawg, whoa," I said, holding my hands in the air to block the unwanted view.

"Well that is unpleasant," said Vete.

"Now this is something you don't want happening," said Hunter.

Ignoring what the rest of us were concerned with, Hunter poked Larry with his gunblade again.

This time Larry said, "ouch! That hurts!"

"Yer completely unprotected like a turtle out its shell," said Hunter.

"Turtles die outside their shell," I said.

"Precisely the point," said Vete.

"Yo so unlike the turtle on the fence post, this turtle did get there on his own yo," said Terminator.

"A ninja turtle without the shell," I said.

"Ha-ha," said Larry.

"Now how long you gon' be immodest in frona these here ladies?" asked Hunter.

"Alright. Alright," said Larry, "so I'm not completely sure this is a dream. Maybe just a weird hallucination from drugs or at the worst I'm in a science tube being fed stimulation."

"Like that one movie trilogy where people dodge bullets," I said.

"Yeah, something like that," said Larry.

His armor returned solid, evidenced by the sound of Hunter's gunblade hitting Larry's breastplate.

43

"Now you have protection again," said Hunter.

The next few minutes Hunter asked us all questions. None of us dared to lie. The girls were asked simple 'yes' or 'no' answer questions to which they either nodded or shook their heads to give the answer.

"That," said Hunter at the end, "was the easiest lesson."

"That's it?" I asked.

"Yo what's next, yo?" asked Terminator.

"That's it," said Hunter, "now to the city to test yer righteousness."

Vete wasted no time taking to the sky, but Hunter grabbed his leg and told him we were going to walk together as a group. I hovered along in the back of the line while the group walked. The farther we got from the giant tree, the less dense the forest became. I was amazed by all the colorful plants I had never seen before. The exotic flowers were what mostly caught my attention, partly because they were the only things which were not brown or green. Even though there were no animals or insects, the forest ground was not littered with dead leafs. Actually, I did not see any dead thing in the forest. Streams also caught my attention. One stream in particular reminded me of my thirst and so I floated away from the group towards the stream, thinking I would take a quick drink and return to the group. I touched ground, knelt down, cupped my hands and took a drink. The water was superb. It was the best water I had ever tasted.

My tastebuds screamed for more and I was about to put my face to the water when a voice behind me asked, "Do you remember the story of Gideon's army?"

It was Vete.

I got up, floated again and looked over my shoulder. "I remember," I said.

The thirst was gone. In part of Gideon's story, the soldiers were tested at a stream. Those who drank from it by cupping their hands to the water and bringing the water to their face while they looked around passed the test, but those who drank from the water like dogs did not become part of Gideon's three-hundred. Vete walked to the stream, cupped his hands and took a drink.

"That's the best water I've ever had in my life," he said. He started to walk back towards the group, but then stopped. "Something's not right," he said.

"You want more water?" I asked, "yeah. I know. That's why I about had my face in it." I started to float away, but I was floating so slow I thought I was not moving at all. "Um," I began, "I can barely move." I tried to land, but I felt like I was not descending at all. My heart began to race.

"My body is being slowed, too," said Vete.

There was a splash in the stream and I managed to see five or six small clear hands extend from the water and wrap around Vete. His body could not respond fast enough to struggle as he was being pulled towards the stream.

"Vete!" I yelled.

His eyes were wide at first, but then his calm look returned.

"Tekon," he said, "I think I've figured this out. The water tastes great, but is filled with a paralyzing agent. We didn't drink enough to become fully paralyzed, but we are moving incredibly slow. The purpose of the paralyzing agent is so that we can't run away and also so that we can't break through the water. These water arms are pretty weak and they're not fast, but we're being slowed down, so we can't resist."

"So then what are we gonna do!?" I asked.

The sky filled with hysterical laughter from a high pitch male voice. "What to do!? What to do!?" said the voice, followed by more hysterical laughter. "He's trapped!" said the voice, "and by the time you're able to move at regular speeds, poor Prince White over here will be long gone and drowned! However! If you wish to save your dear prince, you must uuuse, your first wish!"

Vete was only a few feet from the water's edge.

"What?" I asked.

"As a CBA," Vete spoke quickly, "you get one wish, however as chosens we get three wishes. Each individual wish has certain rules to it. For the first wish, the wish must benefit someone else more than the person making the wish. Tekon. I need you to wish for me to be able to move faster than the human eye can see. That will grant me extreme speed as well as side effects such as speedy recovery and a hyper immune system which can fight off the paralyzing agents in my body much faster."

Vete's feet were in the water.

"Oh! Clever boy!" said the voice, followed by hysterical laughter again.

"Alright!" I said, "I wish for him to be-"

"WAAAAIIIITTTT waitwaitwaitwait WAIT!" boomed the voice, "You have to have your sword out first," the voice wined.

"How do I-"

"Quote a verse!" Vete interrupted me this time.

"Oh! Um. Jesus Wept!"

The laser sword hilt formed in my right hand. I pressed the button. Vete was up to his knees in the water.

"Ooo!" said the voice, "what is it?"

"A laser key sword," I said, "with water and an unknown material for the x. Now. I wish for Vete to be able to move faster than the human eye can see!"

47

The x on my weapon began to glow in white light and my weapon painfully yanked my arm up and pointed at Vete. Vete also began to glow in white light and then disappeared. Hysterical laughter filled the air again and Vete appeared in front of me.

"You thought you'd figured me out, did you little mouse?" mocked the voice. More hysterical laughter.

"Couldn't find him, huh?" I asked Vete. He shook his head.

"Your new speed still makes you a turtle compared to me," said the voice with yet another laugh.

"This dude's like a hyena," I mumbled. Then it hit me. I had heard this voice before and I remembered exactly where. "Vete!" I began, "this is one of the voices I heard in that room!"

"Then does that make me the boy they want to kill?"

"What are you two mumbling about?" asked the voice.

"Let's go," said Vete, "there's no point in staying here. This guy wanted to single us out and get you to use your first wish and he got that, but obviously he doesn't want to get his own hands dirty in killing me."

"But in getting me to use my first wish he told me how to save you," I said, "Also, why didn't those water tentacles come for me?"

"Because the water wasn't meant for you," said the voice, followed again by hysterical laughter.

"We can think about this later," said Vete, "when we're safe."

"Safe!? Safe!?" boomed the voice, "you will never be-"

"Veeeete!" came a voice in the distance, "Tekoooon!" Terminator.

"Oh look," said the voice, "mighty mouse has come. We'll play again later, kiddos." His last hysterical laughter faded away quickly.

Terminator wobbly flew into view. "Yo where'd you guys go, yo?" he asked me.

Looking at him, I could tell it took all he had to not stare into the gaping hole in my hood.

I answered, "we were-"

"Following this trail of flowers," said Vete.

I guessed the paralysis had worn off because I turned quickly to him. He was pointing to the stream, but when I looked I instead saw a trail of black and blue flowers with various petal shapes and accent colors. Vete's outer layer of clothing did not become transparent at all.

Hunter was not happy when we finally got to the group again at the edge of the forest. Hunter stood on the line where grass met concrete. The triplets were throwing berries at each other by a tree and Larry was watching

49

them from another tree. The city was indeed marvelous. The first site to catch my eye was a sky scraper in the far off horizon with a giant TV screen. As the tallest building I could see, I assumed it to be the center of the city. There were other tall buildings as well, but sizes decreased the farther away they were from the center. Behind Hunter was a one-story antique shop.

"Look who finally decided to show up, y'all," said Hunter with his arms crossed. The girls and Larry walked over. "Just 'cause y'all two are chosens don't mean you get no special treatment."

Vete looked at me and I could easily tell the grammatical error of the sentence was on his mind, but having been raised in the south I thought nothing of Hunter's use of a double negative.

"Now where y'all been?" he asked.

"Following a trail of blue and black flowers," said Vete before I could answer. Again he lied, but again his armor did not reveal himself. How was this happening? Hunter stared at Vete for a while.

"You truly are a powerful boy," he finally said.

Chapter 3

Hunter had led us to the center of the city in front of the tallest skyscraper. We saw many buildings, streets, cars and subway entrances along the way, but not a single person in sight. There were empty casinos, empty banks, empty stores, empty houses and empty restaurants. The entire city had a population of eight. Hunter stood in front of the door to the skyscraper facing us. It was a revolving door. Inside was the tile floor of what appeared to be a hotel lobby. We stood in a semi-circle around him. He looked at each of us and disappeared in the same fashion Vete did earlier in the forest. There were no smokescreens or mirrors or flashy distractions. He either teleported or he could move just as fast as Vete, if not faster. His face reappeared on the giant screen above.

"Let's play hide-n-seek," boomed Hunter's voice. It echoed in the empty city. "I'm hidin' somewhere in this here city," he continued, "so come find me. Oh, and one more thing…"

It was marvelous what happened next. The city came to life. Engines started, fountains began to flow and people appeared out of nowhere. What was once an empty sea of metal, glass, cement and asphalt had then become an ocean full of life. I looked at the screen, but it was showing an ad for a drink.

"The city will test our breastplate of righteousness," said Vete.

"So our righteousness is going to be tested?" asked Larry, "this is stupid. I'm out. If righteousness is going to be tested then I've already failed."

The three girls walked off to a nearby clothing store, Always 21. Terminator's stomach growled loudly and he headed off towards a restaurant which served only chicken and had cow mascots with signs telling people to eat more chicken.

"Tekon," said Vete behind me, "I'll go look for Hunter."

"Yeah, man," I said.

"How's he gonna find him?" asked Larry.

"Have faith," I responded, "you got any money on you?"

He shook his head. "My wallet flew off with my pants," he said.

"Same here," I responded, "but Terminator and the girls went to stores, so maybe they still have money."

I was about to take my first step towards the store when Larry and I heard a scream. I looked in the direction it came from and something pushed me down.

"Hey!" Larry screamed.

I got up and dusted myself off, but Larry had already disappeared into the crowd, chasing the person. Terminator also came into view chasing someone. Someone else was chasing Terminator. The three girls were out of the store and had made their way to me without a word, but one girl did look at me.

"Yeah," I said as if I read her mind, "let's go find out."

I rose to the air to try and catch a view of Terminator. The girls followed. I heard police sirens and watched as cars blazed down the street in the same direction Terminator had gone. We followed them in the sky.

"Did you girls get anything?" I yelled over my shoulder.

As I assumed, there was no response. Of course, the lack of shopping bags in their hands should have answered my question before it was asked. One girl did look at me. I believed she was the same girl from before. The car chase continued, but we stopped at an alley where different police cars were cornering someone. The car doors opposite the alley were opened with police positioned behind them, guns drawn. We slowly landed behind the distracted police. Terminator was being held at gun point by someone wearing a black bean mask, a black jacket and blue jeans. The other guy beside him wore the same outfit.

"Nobody move!" yelled the first crook, "or I'll shoot the kid!"

"Yo man I ain't the one you really wanna shoot, yo," said Terminator, "yo that's just a waste of ammunition. What you really wanna do is-"

"Shut up!" said the first crook.

"There's no way out, man!" said the second crook, "we ain't gonna make it!" The second began to pace around, tapping his gun to his head.

"Will you shut up, man!?" said the first, "I'm trying to think. Hey. climb that fire escape over there. Then, I wantcha to point the gun at the kid. Then he'll climb up and I'll climb up after him."

"Don't move!" yelled a cop, but they proceeded with the plan.

Those events were told to me later by Terminator, because the moment I saw him held at gunpoint I was brought back to the scene at the bank. I was shot at point blank range. I could almost feel the bullet pierce my side again. Reagan kicked and screamed. No one did a single thing to stop him. I hated them. I would always hate them. Those people who stood there and did nothing as Reagan was taken away. But then, what was I doing while Terminator was being held at gunpoint?

When I came to, Terminator was climbing the fire escape and a crowd had gathered in front of me. The adults' attention was drawn to the alley, but the kids' attention was drawn to me. I watched a little girl tug at her father's pant leg to get his attention. The moment she turned her head to her father, I rose to the air and landed on top of the building the crooks were climbing the fire escape of. I looked down at the girl and her father. He was wearing a black suit. Another man in a black suit came up behind him after the little girl was distracted by a toy the father gave her. The man came from the father's back left, moved his right arm over the father, then his left and kept walking. The father dropped and I knew what had just happened. He was assassinated via wire killing. With the father being in the back of the crowd and the girl distracted, no one saw, but I did. What kind of city was this?

A gun clicked behind me.

"Who are you? Some kind of anime freak?" It was the voice of the man who first climbed the ladder.

"What are you doing!?" shouted the crook below, "point the gun at the-!"

His voice stopped and was followed by a thud. I turned around in time to see the man on the roof drop as well. Blood poured from his head as I walked to the ladder.

"Tekon!" said Terminator. He quickly climbed the remaining rungs.

"Wait! You can't leave yet!" screamed a male voice below.

I looked to see a police officer climbing the ladder. He was Hispanic, had black curly hair and a slight muscular build. A scream below was heard. Someone must have noticed the dead father.

55

"Awe geez," said the officer, "wait right there!"

He was down the ladder in a flash and ran out to the crowd. We flew to the top of the skyscraper in the center of the city and stayed there, scanning the skies for any signs of Larry. There was a round metal table with round metal benches built into it on the center of the rooftop. A deck of playing cards sat atop the table. Terminator told me the story about the two crooks who robbed food from the restaurant and jewelry from the customers. The girls sat silently at the round table as we listened to Terminator's story. One girl, who I assumed to be the same girl from before, looked at me occasionally. We decided to feed our stomachs. Terminator would find a quick job he could perform in the city while I would search for Hunter. The girls were to remain atop the skyscraper should Vete or Larry return.

In the skies I started noticing more chaotic events occurring. A bank robbery on one street, a brawl in an alley and another car chase were the events which caught my eye. When sundown was near, while I flew in the northern end of the city, I flew over a small white church and heard the voice in my head.

'I hope this first night is not too terrible for you, Tekon.'

I had not heard the voice in a while, so I stopped in the air and looked around. I could see no one. Ambulance sirens blared in the distance. Cars honked more frequently.

"Where are you!?" I shouted.

"Tekon!" yelled Vete below.

He was standing at the red front double doors of the white cathedral-like church wedged between two three-story buildings. I flew to him.

"How's the search going?" I asked him.

"I want you to see something," was all he said as we walked through the doors.

Immediately I stepped into the sanctuary of the church. There was hardwood flooring. The pews were wooden with red cushioning. On the far end of the sanctuary, on the platform, was a wooden cross with a baptismal tank under it. The wooden podium on the altar had a white cross on it. Stained glass windows lined the side of the sanctuary. To my right was a staircase leading down. Above it was a sign which read "Fellowship Hall". To my left was another staircase leading up. There was no label above it. Usually, when I was in a new place, my first instinct was to explore, but this time I would have to wait, because Vete was walking away. I followed him.

"Professor said that Class B Angels are to eventually replace regular angels," said Vete, "but what all does a guardian angel do besides protect?"

We stopped a few rows back behind two ladies sitting at a pew praying. One had grey hair in a bun with some streaks of black. The other had long jet-black hair. They were both Hispanic.

"The elder one, the grandmother, could die at this very moment," said Vete, "the doctors said that it's just her time. She could die in her sleep, die when she's eating, or any other time. The younger one, has cancer. She, too, could die at any time. Their family can't afford treatment or a stay in the hospital or even a funeral."

I began to feel sorry for them. They were both living on borrowed time. Something boomed outside and shook the building, but I paid it no attention.

'Tekon, please be somewhere safe,' echoed the voice softly in my head.

If the city was any indication of twenty-first century America, there were no safe places.

"Come meet them," said Vete.

We walked over to the pew on the second row in the right column. The elderly woman noticed us first. She was wearing a grey dress with white flat shoes and a white under-shirt. The younger was wearing a blue long-sleeve shirt with a black pencil skirt and blue high heels. Her hair was down in curls. The glazed eyes of the elder pierced my hood as if she knew exactly where my eyes were.

"Are you a death angel?" her slow, withered voice asked me.

The younger turned suddenly, a look of horror in her eyes at the sight of me.

"No," she cried, "just give her a little longer! Please!"

"It's alright, dear," said the elder, holding the hands of the younger woman in her lap.

I looked at Vete. "We're Class B Angels," he said, "this is part of what angels do."

I crossed my arms. "I'm not so sure removing the soul from the body, A.K.A. killing, is in our jurisdiction, nor what we were chosen for."

Vete shook his head. "That's not what I mean," he said, "we're here to-"

The front doors busted open and cursing came inside. The younger woman shrieked. I turned to see seven men. One was caucasian, two were black, three were Asian and one was Hispanic. Each wore black tank tops and black jeans with a viper tattoo on their left shoulders.

"Gabriella," shouted the front Hispanic man who I assumed to be the leader, "where you been, baby!?"

Gabriella jumped from her seat and ran to the man, but the look on her face showed only fear. Words were exchanged in Spanish. From the looks of it, a plea was being made, but the plea must not have worked because he grabbed her arm and tossed her aside where the remaining thugs laughed and began to surround her. The Hispanic man walked over to us and I could see the bulging muscles in his arms.

"If you're not here to escort my soul," said the elderly woman, still sitting in her pew, "then perhaps you are here to protect?"

"What are you supposed to be?" The Hispanic man was standing near us.

"What do you want?" asked Vete.

The man was a head above me. "You supposed to be some kinda angel, pretty boy?" he asked with a chuckle. "That's cute," he continued, "step aside if you know what's good for you."

"Why'd you toss her in the pew?" I asked.

The man looked at me and squinted his eyes. "Freaky," he said, "now move aside. I got grown folk business with the lady."

"Answer my question," I said.

The girl started yelling "No! Stop!"

I looked to see four men holding her limbs while the black and white man seemed to be playing rock-paper-scissors and I did not have to be a genius to guess what the prize for winning was.

"Hey!" I shouted and bolted in their direction, but the simple sound of a gun being cocked stopped me before the man ever told me to stop right there. I turned around and sure enough his pistol was pointed at me.

"Draw!" I heard an Asian man say.

"Dag nabit, Gus! You were supposed to go with rock!" said the caucasian man.

"Shawn! I always go with paper first. You know I been goin' with paper since the third grade."

"Well, you know what Gus, it's time for change. Go with rock this time."

"You said that 'cause I'm black. And no, I will not go with rock this time. After paper I always go with scissors."

"Why?"

"Because starting with paper shows that I'm intellectual and like to know a situation first. Then scissors to show that I know when to strike and with precision. THEN rock to show that I can lay the hammer down."

"Like Hammer Time?"

"Is that because I'm black?"

"Just get on with it!" shouted another Asian man.

The Hispanic man rolled his eyes and said, "newbies."

Vete appeared between the man and I, hit his gun out of his hand with one hand and palmed the Hispanic man in the chest with his other hand. The speed at which Vete performed these simultaneous actions created enough force to send the gun flying to the white ceiling and get stuck in it as well as the man hurtling towards the podium. I turned around and bolted towards the thugs. The four who were restraining the woman each pulled out a handgun with their free hand, but I did not stop.

Instead I said, "Jesus wept," and activated my weapon.

The black and white man both screamed like girls and fled the building.

I heard one shout, "I told you, Shawn! You don't do this kind of stuff in a church! I am not messing with angels and demons!"

The other shouted, "God don't let me die for this man's sins!"

Gun shots were fired at me, but I hardly felt anything. When I reached the first thug I did an upward diagonal slash from my right side. My sword hooked the man's neck and I spun and slung him over me into the ground. More gun shots were fired. I turned around and stepped on something. I looked down to see I had stepped on a bullet. The man I had thrown to the ground started to move. I guess I hooked his jaw instead. The three other men fired their last rounds at me. One bullet actually went in my hood. I took it out and flicked it away. Horror filled their faces.

"He can't die," said the other black man as he started walking backwards, "he's like her!"

He turned and ran. The others followed suit. Who was he talking about?

"Get back here cowards!" screamed the Hispanic man.

He was in front of the altar walking towards the elderly woman. By now Gabriella was standing by me. She shouted something in Spanish and the man responded. Police sirens blared outside the church doors.

"We'll finish this later, sweetheart," said the man before he ran towards a lower window. Just as he was about to jump through the window, Vete appeared in front of him, grabbed him by his neck and slammed him to the wall beside the window. At the same time, Gabriella screamed his name, Alejandro. The church doors busted open and officers stormed the building. I recognized one officer as the same from the alley. Vete disappeared and I flew out through a window which was conveniently open. From the sound of glass shattering below, Alejandro escaped as well.

It was night time. Sirens and gunshots were backdrop. Vete was standing on air above the church's bell tower. I flew up to him and remembered our conversation from earlier.

"What were you talking about back there?" I asked him.

"Those women saw me at first as an angel of life," he said, "and when you came they saw you as an angel of death. Did any of those women look familiar to you? Did any of those criminals or anyone else you've seen in this city look familiar to you?"

"No. Why?"

"I think there's another purpose to this city besides just testing our righteousness."

"Which is..?"

"I haven't quite figured that out yet."

"Well let's get back to finding Hunter and maybe then we can ask him. Speaking of which, what was that back there in the forest?"

"I don't know. Someone with incredible power."

"Yeah that, too, but I'm talking about you lying and getting away with it. How come your armor didn't go all ghost-like?"

"I have layers of armor. My helmet, breastplate and girdle are all the same thing: my robe. So really I'm wearing three robes, thus creating three layers of armor."

"Oh. Wow. Clever."

"What about you? You mentioned when we first met that the pants and gloves were given to you, and I'm guessing your cloak is your helmet, so where's your shield and girdle and breastplate?"

"Well my breastplate is a under my cloak and my shield is on my back. Where's your shield?"

"My shield is an invisible dome around me."

"Oh really? Cool. So what about your layers? You lied twice in the forest. How do you get your layers back without confessing the truth?"

"Repent. I don't plan on lying frequently. Be sure your sins will find you out. I don't plan on keeping our events in the forest a secret forever."

"Yeah why didn't you tell Hunter anyways?"

"Because I don't trust him."

"Why don't you trust him? He's an angel."

"And what do you think that voice was?"

"A demon?"

"This is the Class B Angel headquarters. Demons couldn't be here running loose."

"Not necessarily. I played a game once where humans were trained as mercenaries to combat monsters and sorceresses. The students were called seeds and in the forest section of their garden, that's what their school was called, they let monsters run loose. It was the training room. We're in a training room, and in the forestry area we encountered a demon."

"But Tekon, you said so yourself you heard the voice before in the first room you saw with no clouds. Where people were talking about killing a boy."

I crossed my arms. "Oh," I said, "that's right. ... So either not every angel here can be trusted or a demon has infiltrated CBA HQ and is working with people or angels, or a group of demons have infiltrated CBA HQ and one of them messed with us. But what about other people? Couldn't they do that, too? I mean you have extreme super speed now. What if someone used a wish that granted someone power over water and extreme super speed and either illusion or power over space?"

"There's a better chance of getting struck by lightning twice and surviving to win the lottery than that theory, Tekon. I'm sticking with corrupt angels."

"Hey man, just givin' out ideas. And if you don't trust angels, then who do you trust? 'Cause people are corrupt, too."

"I trust you, because we arrived here at the same time and I've been with you since shortly after you woke up."

"Oh, well, thanks."

"We should get back to the group."

"Yeah. From the sounds of it, this city is going crazy."

When we arrived at the sky scraper, Larry still had not returned. Terminator greeted us with chicken sandwiches, chicken nuggets and bottles of water. He handed me a wad of cash to put in one of my pockets, calling me the bank while we were there.

"How'd you get the money?" I asked.

Terminator adjusted his glasses and told me about how the customers and employees thanked him for returning the stolen money and jewelry. The customers gave him money and the store owner gave him the equivalent in coupons for free nuggets and sandwiches with a bottle of water. He used the coupons to get us our meal. There was a sandwich, a box of nuggets and a bottle of water on the table untouched. It must have been for Larry. Just where was he? I laid down after my meal and looked up, but there were no stars nor moon in the clear night sky. Screams became a constant down below and prevented me from sleeping, so I peeked over the edge with the rest of the group to see just what was going on in the city below. It was chaotic. Cars began to explode, windows were shattered and people were murdered. We watched from safety atop the skyscraper while all hell broke loose in the city below. The later the night became, the less the girls could watch until finally they turned away, but the sounds were inescapable. They put their hands to their ears and crouched down in the fetal position, but I could tell it did not help. After ten o'clock I began to think maybe Larry had been killed for good, if he was down there, or perhaps he was in hiding. Although, if I was bullet-proof at the church, then was he? An hour later I could no longer watch the horrors which flooded the streets. I could handle seeing streets covered in blood, bullets filling the air, shops being destroyed, cars blown up or on fire or chasing other cars, but seeing cannibalism in real life was the last straw for me.

When I turned away from the hell below, I saw the girls sitting with their arms wrapped around their legs and their heads in their knees. If they could sleep, I thought, they would not hear anything, but then again, who could sleep through all the cries of hell? The city was definitely not heaven. It should have been named Hell On Earth.

At midnight, Hunter's voice boomed from speakers below and said, "day one and y'all cain't find me. 'Bout now y'all should be some place safe alright. Probly hidin' from the crazies, am I right? When you see crazy comin', cross the street!"

No one left the skyscraper to actually see if it was his face on the screen or not. We were all just fine assuming it was, despite whatever sayings there were about assumptions.

"Now come tomorra," he continued, "the city'll be the peaceful utopia like when y'all first got here until the sun starts comin down. Once it reaches its apex, utopia time is over and it gets worse an worse as y'all done seen. Don't be scared now. For greater is He that is in you, than he that is in the world."

'Stay calm, Tekon,' echoed the soft, gentle voice in my head, 'you will make it through.'

Helicopters, planes and blimps were all shot down and crashed into buildings, houses and people. At one point in the night I had turned my head to see if Vete and Terminator were still watching, Terminator had his face to the ground, but Vete was still watching. Beside Vete's head, on a building farther away, I watched people jump to their deaths. Hunter's voice was not heard the rest of the night.

No one slept. No one would forget.

The phrase 'darkest before dawn' was more true to me in the city than in any other situation in my life. The sounds I heard throughout the night were inhuman, but at the first light of dawn, there was silence. I could not believe my ears. After hours and hours of in-human, hellish cries among other sounds of destruction, there was utter silence. I slowly crawled to the ledge where Vete was. The moment the sun began to rise there was a flash of light. The light was too bright for me and caused me to see spots, but I ignored them and looked into the city until my eyes re-covered, not believing what I was seeing. The city was spotless. It was clean. There were no blown up cars, no blood soaked streets, no dead bodies, no shattered glass, no empty gun shells or empty guns. It was as if the previous night had never occurred.

"How did that happen?" I asked.

"It all just disappeared, in a flash of light," said Vete.

"Yeah I see that," I said as I rubbed my eyes.

Later in the morning, Terminator sug-gested we look underground. I could only imagine what happened in the subways and sewers at night. Vete instead said he would search underground and Terminator and I should search the above ground in case he missed a spot or if Hunter changed hiding places, but, just as we were about to depart, I felt a tug on my arm. I turned my head to see the girl, no, the girls standing by each of us guys. The girl by me was the same girl, I assumed, as before. I looked into her hazel eyes and knew exactly what she was feeling. We were not staying another night in the city, and they wanted to help. Larry still had not returned, so we spread the playing cards on the table in a pattern which read, "BACK AT NIGHT." While Vete and one of the triplets searched the subways, Terminator and a triplet would search the recreational sector while the other triplet and I would search the suburbs.

The girl and I arrived in a gated community where the smallest house was two stories and had a circular window on the second floor. All the houses had a garage, porch, separate front yards with a tree and shared backyards. We walked along the sidewalks, peering through windows as we went. After a while a police car drove up to us. Inside was the same officer from the alley and the church. He looked directly at me.

"Hello, sir," I said.

"Sir do you live here?" he asked.

"No, sir," I said, "we're looking for someone."

"What's their name?"

"We only know his first name, Hunter. He's tall, big build, wears camo a lot, brown hair."

"Sir, I'm gonna have to ask you to get in the back seat. And what about you, miss? Do you live here?" She shook her head. "Alright, I'll need you two to come with me."

I sighed. "Yes, sir."

I opened the car door, but the girl grabbed my other arm exactly how Reagan did which made me freeze. I was brought back to the scene at the bank. The memory played in my head like a horror film.

When I came to, the officer was standing next to me.

"I'm not gonna tell you again to get in the car," he said.

I shook my head and said, "sorry. Yes, sir."

I sat in the car and scooted to the far side. The girl reluctantly sat next to me. The officer closed the door for us, walked around to the driver's side, got in and started driving.

"Miss, I'll just drop you off at the gate," he said, "with a warning, but sir, you were present at the church and the alley yesterday and fled the scene before questioning, which is against the law. So I'm gonna need you to stay in the car. Also I'm gonna need you to remove your hood."

I looked at the girl and she looked back at me. "Sir I'd rather not leave her alone in this city," I said, "and I don't plan to."

"Sir, I can charge you for obstruction of justice."

"I'm not a citizen here, wherever here is. And I'm not gonna leave her alone anywhere in this city! What's this city called anyway!?"

"Sir, lower your voice and keep your wings folded in, please."

The mention of my wings snapped me out of my rage. "Why aren't you frightened by my look or surprised by my wings?"

The car stopped and he said, "there was once a kid like you who came to this city, years ago. She's the reason the city is peaceful from sunrise to midday. Before her, there was no flash of light to erase death and start a new day. There was always chaos."

She? The thugs from last night mentioned some girl, too.

"Who was she, sir?"

"She was-" *I got the target, Wooden Shield, in my sights heading northbound on forty-second. No visual on other weapons, but target is assumed to be armed and dangerous. Requesting backup.* The officer pressed a button on his walkie talkie and said, "Torres is in pursuit." He then sighed and said, "look, I'll cut you a deal. The last of your kind, she was a great help to the city. If you can do the same, I'll let you go. You're technically a vigilante, but if other officers see you helping you'll be at the bottom of their priority list. Deal?"

"Deal. Yes, sir."

The officer let us out of the vehicle at the gated entrance, turned his sirens on and was gone. Wooden shield? Could it be Larry?

I looked at the girl and said, "I betchu we're supposed to like, pray or something and Hunter'll appear out of nowhere."

She looked at me. Then she walked away. I followed her along the road leading away from the gated community. The road was lined with fall-colored trees. Brown and orange would fill perhaps thirty yards or so, then red and pink the next, followed again by brown and orange. I think for a moment we forgot about Hunter and the city and just focused on the scenery. When the community was just out of sight from where we were on the winding road, before the nearest sky scrapers could appear above the trees, a hysterical laughter filled the air. I jumped at first and immediately looked around for any source of water. The girl stood closer to me.

"So," came the voice, the same voice from the forest, "you got a girl this time, eh? I expected your twin, but she'll do just fine!" She held my arm. "Awe, how cute!" said the voice, "are you two dating now?"

In a fit of annoyance, combined with pent up frustration and agitation from the previous night, I said, "dude, shut up!"

Big mistake. There was a pause.

"What?" asked the voice, "excuse me? JUST WHO DO YOU THINK YOU'RE TALK-ING TO!?"

The sky turned a sunset-red color and spheres of fire began to fall from the sky.

"You little worm!" screamed the voice, "I'll burn you to a crisp!"

The fireballs were small enough to fit in my hand and fell hauntingly slow, but there were too many over a widespread area. I could not run or fly fast enough to avoid them all, which left only one option.

"Jesus wept."

The girl crouched down as I started hit-ting the fireballs away, but the more fireballs I hit, the faster the remaining spheres fell. After hitting a few away I noticed the x on my right glove was white and glowing.

"Oooo," said the voice, "this is fun! More! More!"

More spheres of fire fell at increasing speeds and completely filled the sky. I began to freak out in my mind, not knowing what to do. There was no way I could keep blocking the fire which fell.

"Okay!" I shouted, "I give up! You win!"

The words tasted sour in my mouth. I was a gamer. Gamers did not quit. We tried again and again, but we did not quit. Only ama-teurs rage-quit, but this was not a game. I did not have more lives and my skill level was nowhere near high enough to survive the on-slaught. The fireballs stopped in the air.

"What?" boomed the voice, "Do my ears deceive me with wax? What did you just say .. you give up!? I'm so disappointed!"

The fireballs disappeared and the sky returned to its normal color.

"Little girl," said the voice, "do you, take this man, to be your knight in leather armor, 'till eternal death take his soul?"

"What?" I asked.

"Quiet, now. It's the lady's turn to speak. She's i-n-d-e-p-e-n-d-e-n-t. Do you know what that means? Make her feel a-p-p-r-e-c-i-a-t-e-d. Do you know what I mean?"

There was a pause.

"She doesn't talk. At least not since I've known her."

"Oh really? This is even more entertain-ing!"

I ignored whatever he said next and fo-cused on finding a means of escape.

"Tekon!" His voice boomed.

"What?"

"Strike her down."

"What!?"

"Do it! Do it now!"

"No!"

"NOW!"

"NO!"

"You dare defy me!?"

"I don't even know you!"

"Oh! Where are my manners? I'm," his voice then dropped to a very low pitch boom, "your worst nightmare." A low pitch hysterical laughter filled the air and slowly rose to its normal higher pitch.

As he laughed, I grabbed the girl's arm and we took to the sky, but once we were above the first tree, I saw a small translucent orange sphere fall right in front of my face. I instinctively folded my wings in front of me and they became my saving grace. The sphere exploded and flung us back down. I recovered and landed on my feet in time to catch the girl.

"Well done! Well done!" said the voice, "bravo! Now for something harder!"

"I protected her from fireballs, took an explosion for her and caught her when she fell! What more do I-"

"DIE for her!" Hysterical laughter.

Death was hopefully not going to be necessary.

"If I use my second wish, will you let us go?" The laughter stopped. I looked at the girl. She was making glances between me and my weapon. "Oh, to get your sword out you just quote a Bible verse. Um, as for wishes we get three wishes."

"Correction! Chosens get three wishes. Regulars get only one."

"What's up with that? Anyways, can I use a wish and you let us go?'

Hysterical laughter. "When will you learn that it's not all about you, boy?"

I sighed. "Dude, could you please just leave us alone?"

There was silence. I waited a while, took a step and still there was silence.

When we had gotten back to the sky scraper, Larry was there waiting with the rest of the group. He raised an eyebrow and crossed his arms upon seeing us fly in together.

"And just where have you two been?" he asked.

"I could ask you the same question," I retorted, "where were you last night?"

I stayed in the air just beyond the sky-scraper. The girl landed and joined the group around the table. They were playing some game with the cards. Larry's shield and helmet were set off to the side.

"What are you, my nanny? What were you and your boyfriend doing in the forest?" he asked, annoyed.

I crossed my arms and said, "whoa, dude, first off, I don't roll that way. Second, we saw hell on Earth last night and you were nowhere to be seen. Sorry I'm curious as to your whereabouts. I was beginning to think you were dead."

"Oh, you really care?" Sarcasm.

"Dawg, what's wrong with you?"

"Hey! I'm not your 'dawg' and I'm not the one with a problem here."

"Obviously you are. Just what happened to you?"

"It's none of your business what happened to me!'

"So something did happen."

"Just drop it, Tek."

"It's Tekon."

"Well you're Tekon me off."

"Dude, that was lame, and uncalled for."

He jumped up on the ledge and his beady green eyes peered into my hood. We were eye level. "So what if it is? You gonna do somethin' about it, Tek?"

"Dawg, calm down, get out my face witcho hatorade, and just sit relax."

I did it again. Sometimes when I talked my mind thought of two phrases at once and parts of my sentences would not make sense or I would slur words together. It would happen when I got riled up. I once told someone to stop downcrizing me, mixing the words 'downsizing' and 'criticizing' together.

"You're not the boss of me."

"Why are you so angry right now?"

"Why don't you mind your own business!?"

"Dude I'm just-"

Vete's hand appeared between us. He was standing above us horizontally.

"We can stand sideways?" I asked in amazement.

"You're getting too loud," he said and flew off.

I looked at Larry and said, "Dude, we're just glad you're okay. That's all."

I flew past him and joined the group.

We had lunch again from the chicken restaurant which gave Terminator the coupons. After lunch we discussed the sections of the city we had covered and what possible locations were left, assuming Hunter did not change positions. Larry did not speak. He sat in silence as the rest of us discussed. Between the seven of us, we had covered the entire city almost. Of course, only a few of us actually went into buildings to search for Hunter. We just peered through windows, mostly. Of course, not going into buildings greatly hindered our search, but Vete had been in almost every building in the city already.

'Have you looked inside Babel Hotel yet?' The soft, gentle voice echoed in my head.

"Hey guys," I said, "what about Babel Hotel?"

All eyes turned to me and my stomach wanted to vacate the premises.

"Has anyone looked in this building?" asked Vete.

No one had. Of course Hunter would be right under our noses. Oddly enough, we began to feel extremely fatigued after considering Hunter being inside Babel Hotel. I assumed it was from the lack of sleep. It happened gradually as we talked. First we were holding our heads up, then leaning on each other, then talking with our heads down. Once we discussed Hunter being under us, our heads hit the table and our eyes closed. I placed my right hand on the center of the table before I passed out.

When I next awoke I was surrounded by maroon. There was no floor and therefore no distinction between up and down, which terrified me at first. My heart raced.

"Calm down, neophyte," came a male's deep, rough voice.

"Who are you?" I asked.

"All you need to know is that my name is Vadallat and you have the honor of being my conduit."

"Conduit? For what?"

"I've told you all that you need to know. Your body shall serve me well. Once you become more spiritually potent, we shall meet again."

The maroon faded away and I was at the skyscraper again, my head still on the table. I was used to having bizarre dreams before. I dreamt every night, but the previous dream was very vivid. The sun was setting.

I jumped up and shouted, "guys!"

The rest of the group woke up. The group stretched and yawned, but sight of the setting sun quickly reminded them of what we had to do.

"Before we go," said Vete once everyone was ready, "you need to learn how to draw
your swords. In the worst case scenario, things
are ten times worse inside buildings at night
than outside. To draw your sword, you'll need
to quote a verse from scripture."

Larry chuckled. "I don't need to quote
scripture to undue my belt," he said.

I shook my head and said, "seriously?
Watson? Seriously?"

"My last name isn't Watson," he said in
annoyance.

"It sure ain't Holmes either. Getcher
mind outa the gutter. I'm talkin' about this: Jesus wept." The hilt appeared in my hand and I
pressed the button.

"And I'm talkin' about this." He undid his
belt buckle and pulled out a thin bendable steel
sword from between his belt and pants.

"Dude! You have a sword in your belt!?"

"Yeah." He tossed a bottle of water in
the air and cut it in half, splashing water on the
ground by his feet.

"Dude. That's pretty cool. Now, once
everyone gets their verses in mind, we can go."

Vete was the first to jump into Hell on
Earth, as we called it. The rest of us were
slightly hesitant, but as the last of the sunlight
was fading, we braved our fears and flew
down. We walked into the hotel just as the last
light of the setting sun disappeared. Gunshots
could be heard outside. A golden chandelier

hung in the center of the lobby. Bellhops in green outfits with gold rims and golden name-plates were seen pushing trolleys and carrying luggage. There was a fountain on the left wall of the lobby with a golden calf spouting water. On the right wall was the concierge area, but it was the grandeur in front of us which held my attention. The marble tile flooring met red carpet with yellow lions. I walked over to the carpet and saw the interior of the skyscraper. The red carpet covered a spiral walkway which went from the top of the hotel all the way down to the bottom I could not see because of the many patios which jutted out from various sections below. A look above revealed the same for seeing the ceiling of the skyscraper. There was clear glass railing along the spiral, but there were no poles. It was as if the entire rail was one long sheet of glass. I noticed the lions went upwards in the carpet.

"Yo," I heard Terminator say beside me. He put his hands on the glass and leaned. "Yo this is tough stuff," he said, "must be bullet-proof, yo."

"214," said Larry behind me. I turned around to face him. "They said a man named Hunter is in room 214. We just gotta walk along the spiral until we get there."

I nodded my head. The walls of the hotel were red and along the spiral were white doors with black numbers. The first door I saw had 000 on it.

We had started to walk when Vete behind us said, "he's not there anymore."

Terminator jumped.

"How do you know?" asked Larry.

"I was just there. He's not there anymore. Come see for yourself," said Vete.

He rose to the air and we followed. Vete led us to the door to room 214. There was a cut from the doorframe to the handle.

"Yo what happened here, yo?" asked Terminator.

"Someone didn't knock," said Larry.

"I wanted the element of surprise," said Vete, "but he was already gone."

Larry opened the door and walked in with me behind him. The room was large. There was chocolate brown carpet in the living room with a rectangular wooden table and four wooden chairs. There was a window with closed curtains on the far wall. On the left wall was a tan leather couch. On the other side, by a white closed door which I assumed led to the bedroom, was a bookshelf filled with various titles. There was a kitchen to the right with marble counters, hardwood flooring, a black microwave, a black refrigerator and a black oven with two electric eyes and two gas eyes. Larry and I looked over the books.

There were many titles in different languages I did not recognize. One book which caught my eye was a grey book with the title, "H.G."

I tried to take it out, but Vete shouted, "wait!" I stopped and looked at him.

"What? Is this gonna lead us to a booby-trapped bat cave or something?" I asked.

He shook his head and said, "or it could be a trap."

"It's a book," said Larry, "not the movies."

"Well yeah," I said, "but look where we are. There's always the possibility that-Larry wait!"

Larry grabbed the book and removed it from the shelf. "See?" asked Larry, "nothing's gonna hap-"

A dart flew out of the bookshelf and I caught it just before the tip reached his neck.

I looked at him and said, "now do you be-?"

Clear white shells quickly rose from the ground and began to encase us, but Vete appeared by me and the next thing I saw was Larry's shell encasing him. The tip of the clear shell was almost closed and he was pounding on it.

"Jesus wept."

I slashed at Larry's shell, but there was only a scratch. I shoved the dart into one of my pockets, held my weapon with both hands and slashed repeatedly. From the sounds of it, Vete was facing the same issues as I with rescuing the others. The clear shells began to glow in a white light as the space inside the shell began to swirl. I shouted and gave it another slash, this time noticing the glow from the white x on my right glove. The shell shattered like glass. Larry fell out and started puking. I looked over to Vete. He stood by four empty clear pods.

"What happened?" I asked.

Vete shook his head and said, "I don't know. I don't know. How'd you get Larry out?"

I looked at Larry on the ground and said, "I don't know."

I looked at the glove on my hand with the white x still glowing.

Larry slowly stood up. "Thank you," he said to me.

"Yeah," I said, "my pleasure. Put the book back before something else happens." Larry nodded his head. "Where do you think they went?" I asked.

"I don't know," said Vete.

I slammed my right palm on the bookshelf and a maroon dome grew from my hand. Again, I was in the maroon atmosphere from my dream.

"Calm down, neophyte," said Vadallat.

"My name here is Tekon," I said, "and I'm guessing last time wasn't a dream, Mr. Vadallat. Who are you? Where am I? Where's Vete and Larry? Where's Terminator and the girls? Where's Hunter?"

"Calm down, neophyte. You're only hallucinating. The others are all in the room with you."

"Really? How did I get hit with a dart?"

"You didn't. You're experiencing a hallu-cination from airborne spores released into the room the moment Larry took the book from the shelf. The trap is a reverse trap. The dart is ac-tually the salvation. The trap was set so that in case Hunter was ever in a dire situation in this room, he would offer the book. That book is very valuable and in the wrong hands capable of mass destruction. The enemy would then try to grab the book, but Hunter would warn them of the trap set up, in which case the enemy would make Hunter get the book. Hunter would get the book and allow himself to be shot with the dart. The dart carries the antidote for the hallucinogen. So while his enemies begin to hallucinate, he can finish them off or escape."

"Oh. Wow. That's pretty smart. So I need to stab myself with the dart then?"

"Good, neophyte. Now go."

"Wait! You didn't tell me where I am, nor how I got here or how to leave."

"When a glove on your arm glows, you gain newfound strength and become able to transport yourself to this pocket dimension where I may communicate with you."

"Ok. How do I leave?"

"I can release you. There is also a timer that counts down on your glove when you are here."

I looked at my glove. Sure enough, there was a timer counting down, but I did not recognize the symbols. "What language is this?"

"The language of my people."

"Wait so are you the one who gave me the gloves and pants?"

"I gave you the gloves, neophyte, but not the pants. Begone."

The maroon disappeared and I was in the room again with the dart in my hand. Larry was standing, book still in his hand, looking at me. I stabbed my thigh and a few seconds later my vision blurred and then recovered. Larry was standing in front of me holding his severely scratched shield up in defense. I looked around and saw there was only Larry and I in the room.

"Vete?" I asked.

Larry peeked his head over his shield and asked, "Tekon? Is that you?"

I looked at him and asked, "where's Vete and the others?"

"Where are you? Guys? Where'd you go?"

"Larry I'm right here."

"Right where? I can hear you, but I can't see you."

"I'm right here in front of you. What happened to all the pods?"

"What pods?"

"The clear pods that just came right out of the ground and swallowed Terminator and the girls. The same pod I rescued you from after Vete rescued me."

"What are you talking about?"

Did I really imagine the pods? "Larry what's the last thing you remember?"

"Well, I remember us walking in here. You grabbed a book, but Vete didn't want you to and said it might be a trap. So I grabbed it and a dart shot out and you caught it, but then you all started to disappear in black smoke."

I guessed I really was hallucinating. How long until the hallucinogens wore off?

The door beside the bookshelf opened. Hunter was on the other side. Behind him I saw Vete, Terminator and the three girls laid out across a bed. He closed the door and walked past me to Larry. He must have thought me to still be hallucinating.

"Tekon?" asked Larry, "are you still there?"

Hunter pulled his fist back as if to punch Larry. I quickly swung my sword between Larry and Hunter as his fist came forward for the punch. Hunter quickly pulled back his fist and looked at me with a curious look. I slashed downward and he dodged. I watched the look in his face change from curious to confused. He stepped back a few steps and I stood between him and Larry.

"Tekon?" Larry shouted.

"I'm still here Larry," I said, "fighting off invisible bad guys."

"Oh," he said, "well what can I do?"

"Stand still," I said.

I lunged at Hunter with a downward slanted slash from my left. He dodged to his right and sent a left jab to my face which I barely dodged by ducking and he skimmed the side of my head. I came back up with a left uppercut and a left knee to his gut. He caught my uppercut with one hand, my knee with the other, lifted me and threw me through the window. When he lifted me, I realized his eyes were closed. Was he doing all this in his sleep? I recovered and stood in the air. The inhuman sounds of the night again returned to my ears. Hunter walked up to Larry again.

"Hey!" I shouted.

I flew as fast as I could to Hunter and slashed. This time Hunter blocked with his gunblade and there was a shockwave from our clash which shook the room around us and even knocked Larry down. Hunter's eyes opened.

"What in tarnation is goin' on?" he asked.

"Is that Hunter?" asked Larry as he stood again.

I jumped back and hovered in front of Larry.

"You tell me," I said.

"I was sleepin' in my room an' then I wake up with you tryin' ta kill me," said Hunter, "wanna explain why you wer tryna kill me? How'd you getcher sword out anyway?"

"We found your room and went in. A book was grabbed, a dart was shot and we hallucinated and you're sleepwalking? Stackin' bodies? Since when do angels sleep? I thought there was no slumber in heaven."

"This ain't heaven. And I need you to put that book back Larry."

Larry shook his head and did as he was told.

"When do the hallucinations wear off?" I asked.

"They'll be fine by sunrise."

"So you were really sleepwalking?"

"The only place slumber don't overtake ya is heaven and hell."

"You were knocking them out and stacking them in your room. I'm supposed to believe you did all that in your sleep? We just had a fight and you even dodged me a few times. How can you do that in your sleep!?"

"Tekon. Don'tchu ferget that angels have better sight and hearin' than you humans do. I can hear the movements of yer clothes even if you hold yer breath."

"Oh, okay. Sonar location."

"Bullseye. Now get some rest inside. Unless you wanna stay out here."

"I'm not sure I feel safe sleeping around you."

"Angels don't need as much sleep out-side of heaven as you do. I'll watch y'all an' make sure y'all don't hurt each other."

"Alright. Yes, sir. Come on, Larry. "

"Am I goin' nuts or is that a pink butter-fly?" asked Larry as I led him to Hunter's room.

I let Larry go in and then closed the door.

"Is there somethin' you wanna say?"

"If this isn't heaven, then that means angels can lie, right?"

Hunter's face turned fierce as he said, "Watchu getin' at, boy?"

"Just considering the possibility, sir."

"You think I'm lyin' to ya, boy?"

"I never said that."

"You might not have said it with yer words, but it sure seems yer implyin' it."

"I'm just finding this hard to believe."

"You cain't believe what I'm tellin' ya? Do you see me sittin' here in my underwear? I'm held to the same laws you are. If I lie, you'll know it and don'tchu ferget it."

"Yes, sir."

I opened the door and walked into the room. There was a king size bed with pearl pink pillows and pearl designs on the comforter from what I could tell. I did not pay attention to any of the other furniture. I just plopped down at the foot of the bed next to Vete who was laid across the foot of the bed. I looked at my glove. The white x was gone, leaving the empty shell behind. I quickly dozed off.

In the morning we stood in a circle atop the skyscraper after eating fruit for breakfast from Hunter's refrigerator. The temperature during the day was just perfect for me. Vete was at my left and the girl was at my right.

We all held hands and Hunter began, "Dear Lord our heavenly Father…"

His voice was replaced by a calm, deep voice. It sounded like my pastor.

"In Jesus' name, amen," said the deep voice.

It had to be my pastor. I opened my eyes. I was still in the hospital bed. To my right was my mother and to my left my step-dad. They formed a circle around me with my pastor and his wife. My pastor had white hair and wore a grey suit. His wife had dark hair and wore a grey outfit as well. They must have just come from some event.

My pastor smiled and asked, "well how ya doin' there Asanté?"

"Fine-how-'bout-you?"

The words came effortlessly and thoughtlessly out of my mouth. My step-dad smiled. Today he wore jeans and a blue shirt.

"He's fine," said my step-dad.

Everyone smiled. After a few moments of talking, everyone left the room so I could get dressed. The moment they left, the pain came in. My side began to inflame. I felt the patched wound and was brought back in my mind to the scene at the bank. I would always hate them, I thought, I would always hate them for doing nothing when Reagan was taken. I had learned, a while back, a trick to relieving pain. I simply had to get my mind off of it. So I focused on getting dressed. There were a pair of jeans, a dark grey shirt and a black light jacket. Any time I moved my right side I was in pain. Putting my shirt on was the most painful part of getting dressed.

When I opened the door to leave the room, there was a dark man in front of me. He had a muscular build, a slight gut and was a little shorter than me. He wore jeans and a blue shirt with white horizontal stripes.

"Dad!"

I forgot the pain and hugged him.

"Hey, son," he said as he hugged me back.

When he let go he asked if I was feeling okay. I told him about the pain in my side. We walked down the hall to my other parents and did the rest of what I call the parental exchange. My mother told me I was going with my dad for a few days and clothes were already packed. She gave me a hug, I said bye to my pastor and his wife and left with my dad. As we left the hospital my dad and I talked about where to eat, what to do in the city, places to go, etc. In the parking garage I followed my dad to a black SUV.

"Asanté!"

The muffled scream was followed by muffled echoes of the same. My step-mom was in the passenger seat. She was lighter than my dad and I, but darker than my mom. Damian opened the door for me. He was ten years old, a little darker than my mom, but not as dark as his mom. He wore a red shirt and jeans.

"Hey, Asanté," he said.

"Monkey!" said Sarah, my younger sister.

She was nine years old and just as dark as her mother. She wore a pink shirt and jeans.

"Hey!" said my other sister, Cheryl.

She was eleven and light-skinned as well. She wore a bright green shirt and jeans. "Did you die!?" she asked.

"Cheryl," came my dad's stern voice.

The look on his face showed he was not pleased with what she just said. I said hello and sat beside my other younger brother, James. He was as light-skinned as Cheryl, wore a bright purple shirt and tan khaki pants. He was engrossed in whatever handheld game he was playing.

"Hi, Asanté," he looked up and said, "can you help me with this?"

He held his game out to me.

"Sure," I said as I put my seatbelt on.

I recognized the game to be one in which a player captured monsters in special balls and summoned them for battle. We went to a restaurant where the servers carried meat on spokes and brought them to the table. There was also an amazing salad bar, or so I heard. I had been wanting to go to the restaurant since I first heard about it years ago and I was finally there. When we had all gotten our salads from the salad bar, we held hands and began to pray over our food. My father led and said, "Dear Lord our heavenly Father, ..."

With those words, I was sent back to fantasy.

Chapter 4

"In Jesus' name, amen," said Hunter. Our second Prayer Life was over. "Howdy, y'all," he continued, "God's great, ain't He?"

We all looked as if we had just woken up.

"No," said Vete, "He is."

Terminator spoke up, "I thought..."

"No," said Hunter, "the boy's right."

Though I lived in Missouri, I was raised in the panhandle of Florida and spent summers in southern Alabama with a grandma who did not let kids sit around all day watching TV. Heat was nothing to me. My freshman year of high school was spent in Missouri and I participated in marching band. The band practiced throughout the summer on a turf football field which was downhill and surrounded by shining metal bleachers. While other students wore shorts, bright colors and carried jugs of water, I was just fine in jeans, dark colored clothing and one iced bottle of water.

The desert was not Florida or Alabama. The moment I stepped off the city's perimeter sidewalk and into the desert a massive wave of heat slapped me in the face. It was as if the perimeter sidewalk created an invisible wall separating the temperatures. The desert was hot, dry and endless. Even with my southern American heat training, my black outfit attracted way too much heat. I could feel my sweat running down my neck, back, chest and stomach. My pants were practically drenched. We noiselessly followed Hunter through the sand. Hunter carried a bag of ice in which all the water bottles were stored. The burning sand got into our shoes and some of us began to fly, but Hunter demanded we walk. He who controlled the water controlled the students, so we obeyed. I looked at Vete at one point and wondered what I would call his new ability. Extreme Speed? Flash Step? Angelic Speed? Angel Speed?

The fun began when the hallucinations started. Terminator was the first and the funniest. He began whispering about flying bats with long tails. Then he started shouting about floating boats and a gorilla eating a palm tree in one hand and an oak tree in the other. He dodged the bats and jumped on the anchors of the boats, which only sent him tumbling down sand dunes. He ran to a cactus screaming, but Hunter stepped in and saved him from a thorny surprise. Larry laughed at all of Terminator's antics. Terminator passed out and Hunter carried him on his shoulder. We no longer walked in single file. The girl, the one who was with me in the city, walked beside me and Vete walked on my other side. Larry began shouting at no one named Timmy. His laughing became erratic then. Vete and I discussed who would hallucinate next out of the group. We both came to the conclusion the girls would simultaneously hallucinate. I looked at the girl beside me to see if she would communicate any disapproval of our discussion, but sure enough she was frolicking with the other two girls. They skipped as if they were in a field of flowers.

"Timmy," said Larry, "stop chasing skirts. You're such a womanizer." Larry chuckled.

I began to focus on not hallucinating. I thought Hunter was leading us through the desert until we all hallucinated from dehydration, but the test was to see if we would keep our peace and not hallucinate. Vete tapped my shoulder.

"Yeah?" I asked.

"The more peaceful you are, the less the sand burns."

"That's it!" I yelled, "sandals of peace!"

My excitement made me lose my cool and it became my turn to hallucinate. I saw people in black cloaks run around weaving hand signs. One stopped in front of me, weaved some more hand signs and two more people appeared in a cloud of smoke.

"Jesus wept."

The three ninjas rushed me. They were hooded so I did not see their face. I swung my sword at Ninja One, who blocked it with a katana. Ninja Two jumped high over Ninja One and flung shuriken at me. I hopped back to avoid the stars, but was kicked from behind by Ninja Three. I used my smaller wings to wrap around the leg of Ninja Three, turned around, spinning Ninja Three with me, and flung Ninja Three into Ninja Two. The two ninjas disappeared in a cloud of smoke. The real ninja's shadow blocked the sun. I instinctively raised my weapon in a defensive stance and blocked something. The real ninja came down and I slashed. A puff of smoke appeared and disappeared just as quickly, revealing a wooden log with burning stickers. I jumped back and folded my wings in front of me to protect me from the explosion, but I stuck my sword behind me as well and felt it impale the real ninja. I heard the real ninja drop to the ground. There were two more real ninjas to deal with.

One stood in front of me and slowly said, "ban, kai."

The ninja's sword became a white tiger. The tiger circled me. As it got behind me I stepped to the side to try and create a triangle formation, not wanting to have my back toward either opponent. The tiger crouched, which drew my attention to it. I heard the ninja clap his hands and turned to see him slam both hands to the ground. The tiger pounced on me. The earth began to shake and I began to sink in the sand, unable to move with the tiger's weight on me. The tiger roared in my face. I pressed the button on my sword, withdrawing the saber. I positioned the hilt under the tiger and pressed the button again. The tiger yelped as the sword went through it. There was a flash of light and the tiger turned back into a sword. I struggled to get out of the sand, but eventually I did. The ninja stood still.

"I recognize that word," I said.

The ninja then clapped his hands once and rushed me. I also recognized the single hand clap and knew I should not let him touch me. I hopped back three times, each hop longer than the previous. Without stopping he picked up his sword and ran his other hand over it from bottom to top. Then he grabbed a second sword from his first sword! It was as if the sword grew a copy of itself! His cloak then turned red with black heart designs. He quickly closed the distance between us and swung both swords across. I blocked vertically, jumped up and palmed the ninja in the face. The ninja fell down and rolled away in time to dodge my stomp. The ninja jumped back high in the air and threw a sword at me. I flew after him, caught his sword, switched grips so I was holding both swords in a backhand fashion and slashed him with both swords. He also switched to a backhand style and tried to block vertically, but my sword cut through his and therefore through him. He disappeared in a cloud of smoke. The third and final ninja was on the ground. I remained in the air above. There was a large device on the ninja's arm. The ninja held up a card and slammed it on the device. A rectangle of light appeared on the ground and out of it rose a ball whose top half was red and the bottom half was white. A black line separated the colors and there was a black circle in the middle of the black line. The ball flew towards me. I flew away from it and it followed me, so my first thought was to fly to the caster to see if the ball would hit him, but the ball was too fast and instead hit me. When it did, a red light shot from the black circle to me and I could feel myself being sucked into the ball. My heart pounded against my chest as I screamed. The next thing I saw were the words:

Fate/.Hack//HorizonArtOnline
Username: Attack on Piece.
Castle Level: 84
Player Level: Nen User
World: Namek
You have 5 minutes until you face the Generation of Miracles. Do you wish to enlist the help of Web Slinger and Dark Knight? Yes No

I did not know what to do. I moved my hand to press "yes." New words appeared:

Congratulations on your search for the 7 Emeralds of Chaos. Beware of dog demons. They capture cards.

Dog demons? What?
'You're doing great, Tekon. Persevere,' the soft, gentle voice echoed in my head.

When I woke up, there was a blank night sky above me. My head throbbed as I slowly sat up. I was still in the desert. Everyone laid asleep around me. When I saw Hunter sleeping with the ice bag as a pillow, my thirst hit me like a jackhammer. I slowly crawled over to him and even more slowly I grabbed a water bottle out of the ice bag without making a sound. I slowly crawled a few feet away from the group and sat up. I practically ripped off the bottle cap and almost drowned myself in water. My coughs woke one of the girls. She looked at me, then at Hunter. She quickly, yet silently, reached in the ice for a bottle and yanked it out. She walked to me, sat down, gently unscrewed the bottle cap and slowly drank her water. No coughs. My previous theory debunked by Vete's, I was left clueless as to why Hunter did not give us water. I looked at the girl and realized even in this silent desert I could not hear her gulps. I could not hear her swallow.

"Why didn't he let us have any water?" I whispered to her.

She shrugged her shoulders. I thought her to be the same girl who was with me in the city.

I looked at the sky and said, "you know, as much as none of this makes sense, I'm glad to be a part of this adventure. It'll make a great story one day. Maybe even a movie. That's what I'll do. I'll write all this down and call it

Class B Angel. No one has to believe it, but it'll be awesome. They say that only one person has ever quit after going through CBA training. I wonder if only one person has ever found Hunter in the city and if those two people are the same person." Her bottle was half empty. "I did use my first wish," I continued, "in the forest. To help Vete. He was caught in a trap and so I wished for him to have speed faster than the eye can see. I think I'll call it Angelic Speed. Or maybe the Latin words for Angelic Speed. Yeah. Latin's cool. Anyways, that voice we heard in the city, it was there in the forest, too. I'd also heard it before then."

"Do you always trust people this easily?" came Vete's voice behind me.

The sound of his voice made me jump. Vete walked past me on the other side.

"How long have you been listening?" I asked him.

He kept walking and said, "long enough."

We got up and followed him.

"Where ya goin'?" I asked.

"To pass this test," he answered.

"Ain't this supposed to test our peace? I thought you said it was about the sand burning our feet?"

"During the day, the more peaceful you are, the less the sand burns and you don't hallucinate. I was the only one who didn't hallucinate, besides Hunter of course, but there's more to this test than that. There's something to do with why Hunter won't give us water, and I think those hallucinations are supposed to reveal something."

"So you think there's something more to this desert just like there was something more to the city?"

"Yes, though I haven't figured out the city's other function, but I have no desire to return to it."

"Yeah what was that back there in the city? With those two ladies?"

"I don't-"

Hysterical laughter filled the air. The girl and I both jumped, but Vete knew this would happen, it seemed.

"Shouldn't you kids be in bed?" came the voice. We looked around, but the sky was clear and there was no one else around us in the desert. "Waitwaitwait. Aren't you the girl from before?"

"What do you want now?" I yelled.

"Don't you take that tone with me, young man!" said the voice, followed by more hysterical laughter.

Vete walked over to me and said, "there's no use running. He could be anywhere."

"Yeah, I tried that in the city with her. It didn't work out too well."

The voice spoke up, "I'm anywhere, I'm everywhere. I'm in your hair, I'm in your underwear!" More hysterical laughter.

"Dude!" I said, "that's just, dude!" I looked at the girl and said, "I'm sorry you were dragged into this." She shook her head. "Just tell us what you want!" I yelled to the sky.

"Quiet!" shouted the voice. Vete started walking away. "And just where do you think YOU'RE going!?"

"Out of earshot," he answered. There was a momentary silence. I thought Vete just said there was no use running away?

"Excuse me?" asked the voice.

"Last time we met," said Vete as he kept walking, "your voice seemed to be coming from everywhere, but when I focused I noticed it was louder in one direction. When I sped to that direction, your voice was being projected from somewhere else."

"I out-sped you, you little runt, now come back here!"

"No! You're just a voice. An annoying voice."

"You brat!"

"Although, it's because of you that I have this newfound power, so thank you, but your constant yapping and crazy laugh is annoying, so I'm just walking away peacefully."

I decided to test this new theory and started flying away in a different direction. The girl walked in a new direction as well, creating a triangle of the three of us.

The voice began to whine, "what? Wha-where are you going?" Then it shouted, "GET BACK HERE!"

I did not think any of us would turn around, but we definitely were not going any further away. A giant wall of fire shot up in front of me from the sand. I turned away from the intense heat and caught the girl. She had flown straight to me. The momentum behind her almost pushed me into the wall of fire.

She held me tight and it was all I could do to get one hand loose and say, "Jesus wept."

I looked around to see we were in a triangle of fire. Each of us were originally at a corner of the triangle. I pressed the button and the girl immediately let go and hovered a few feet away from me. I turned towards the wall and started striking. The sword went through the fire, but did not create an opening for us to go through. I turned around and Vete was in front of me.

"I have a plan," he mouthed.

"Hey!" came the voice, "secrets don't make friends!"

But friends make secrets.

Vete continued mouthing his words, "I'm going to un around is a purple a fir you go to the sit her. Bake the her."

He disappeared and reappeared in the center of the triangle on the sand. The girl and I flew to him.

"What'd you say?" I asked.

"There," said the voice, "that's better! Everyone form a line now, we're gonna play a game!" The girl stood next to me, but Vete walked ahead a few paces and stopped. "Got something to say, oh chosen one?" asked the voice, followed by more hysterical laughter.

Vete said nothing. He disappeared, reappeared, disappeared, reappeared and disappeared continually, all in a blur. I did not understand what was going on until the sand around us began to rise.

"He's..." I started to speak, but stopped when it became harder to breathe. Why was Vete making a sand tornado?

"What?" shouted the voice, "what is this?" The girl flew up and I followed. "Stop that!" shouted the voice, "that's not what we're playing!"

There was no laughter this time. As we flew higher I saw bursts of orange beyond the sand. It was hard to fly straight up, but we both managed somehow though we were ascending incredibly slowly.

The voice spoke, "I'm closing in on you! A circle in a triangle! CT, CT, CT, See tea, sea tea, sea tees ee tease ee tease eat ease eat ease eat ease eat CT CT CT CT."

He stopped talking once we made it to the top. What we saw was something marvelous. I thought Vete was just running around in circles creating a sand tornado, but what I saw in front of me was one Vete deflecting fireballs which were being shot at the tornado from the walls of fire, another Vete striking at the walls and another Vete was shouting at the walls for a reason unknown to me. It was as if there were Vete clones doing their separate activities to try and escape.

"Look who decided to join the party," said the voice.

Another Vete appeared in front of me, flashing in and out as if it were a science fiction hologram. I did not want to blink in case I missed him.

"Dude!" I said, "how fast are you!?"

"Angel Dance," said Vete, "I can create illusions of myself by slowing down at certain places, leaving an after image. Now listen closely because I can't stay long. I can only keep up five illusions for a short time before I have to go back to just four."

When did he learn all this? In the city?

"Alright," I said.

"No means of escape," he continued, "fire rises, and miniature explosions knock me back, even at this speed. I will use my first wish."

"Wait, Vete-" I said.

"Bring out your sword," he interrupted.

"Jesus wept."

I pressed the button and the weapon came out. There was a crackling sound as well from the sand getting caught in the water and burned by the light. I inspected my weapon and it started to glow in a white light. By the time I realized what the glow was for and looked at Vete, it was too late. Vete had already withdrawn his weapon.

"Key to escape," said Vete before he disappeared.

"Oo!" said the voice, "a new power! Use it! Use it!"

"If I use it," I yelled, "will you leave us alone?"

There was a pause before he finally said, "sure."

"Good," I replied.

Unfortunately, I had no idea what my power was or how to use it or activate it. I looked at the girl. She crossed her arms across her chest with her hands in a fist and each fist touching the opposite shoulder. Both of her feet were touching as well.

"Ooh! Charades!" boomed the voice.

"Hey! Hey!" I said, "I got this!"

The girl seemed to be bound. Key to escape. Bound girl. Wait. Duh. My sword was a laser key sword. Emphasis on key! I flew down to the eye of the chaos.

"Hey!" came the voice, "you didn't guess!"

I landed and said, "I got this!"

Weapon in hand, I stabbed the ground as I knelt on one knee. The sword went in pretty easily. I waited.

"What?" asked the voice, "that's it?"

I looked at the girl. She was standing beside me, her hair blowing with the wind. She held out her hand, clenched in a fist as if she were holding something, and twisted her fist. So I turned the key. There was a tremor in the ground. It shook us both and even affected Vete. He crashed into the sand beside me. I looked at him and then up to see the result of the end of his angelic dance. Sand and small fireballs filled the air and fell toward us. It was like a tsunami from the sky. I instinctively took my sword out to block the oncoming doom, but the moment my key was released, the moment everything was just above our heads, the ground beneath us gave way. Actually it was more like a rug being pulled from beneath our feet. Obviously, we fell. It was like watching a 3-D movie in a movie theater. The sand, the fire and the hysterical laughter all came at us in a fashion which made me think I was dreaming again. Of course, the dreaming sensation ended when my stomach reminded me of what was reality. If my stomach could, it would have jumped out of my mouth. The falling fire lit the hole we were in. The soft, cushiony grass saved us. A patch of grass in a dark cave. While I was groping the green salvation, Vete

110

was focused on saving us from the gritty, fiery death above. The patch of grass jutted out from a large hole in the cave. Vete wasted no time getting the girl inside and then me. One moment I was looking at grass; the next I was watching the sand completely disconnect the grassy cliff from the tunnel we were in. The last of the fireballs fell and with it our source of light.

"Well, everyone," I said, "let's grab hands and I'll touch my wings to the wall and lead us out of here." The girl's hand quickly held mine before I finished speaking.

"It'd be easier," said Vete as his hand grabbed mine, "if the person in front keeps their hand on the wall and leads us."

"True. True."

There was total darkness with no light in sight. The cave was damp and smelt so, but it was nice to walk on grass. How did grass grow down here? The girl was in front, then me and then Vete. Vete's hand felt calm and relaxed, which made me calm and relaxed. Later on the girl's hand stopped trembling and her grip on mine loosened. It was a long walk and I started drifting off into daydreams. I thought about how my new power worked, how I would find and save Reagan and what kinds of other Class B Angels I would see. I got to thinking about unanswered questions as well. What were the girls' names? What was the other function of the city? The desert? Did Hunter lie to us about

sleep walking? His actions seemed pretty conscious, but then again there was the height-
ened hearing and sense of smell. Did Hunter
know about Vete's lie? Did Hunter know I used
my first wish? Why was an atheist here? What
did Larry do in the city? Did Vete learn Angel
Dance in the city? Had anyone ever found
Hunter before? Who was the person who quit?
How did Vete know so much if we "died" at the
same time?

My thoughts met an abrupt end when
the girl's hand yanked mine down. I was caught
off guard and a gasp escaped my lips as I fell.
Vete, thankfully, did not fall. He stood on air as
I held on to both his hand and the girl's tightly. I
looked up and was going to thank Vete, but
past him I saw a small white circle. Light. My
heart raced and I flew up, pulling the girl with
me.

"Thanks Vete!" I said as I passed him.

I was quickly pulling him, too, until he let
go. The girl kept my hand in hers and began to
lace our fingers together as she flew beside
me. As the circle grew bigger and brighter, the
cave grew smaller. I accidentally hit one of
Vete's wings with mine. We looked at each
other and folded our wings. I watched his eyes
look down at my hand holding the girl's. I was
glad he could not see the huge smile on my
face. Flying out of the hole was like waking up
from a nightmare. My heart still raced, my vision still blurred and eyes were squinted.

Scared moments before, I was then realizing the event was over.

With the sun above and the green below, I realized we were in the forest again. Even from the height we were at, there was only forest as far as the eye could see. I looked down, but whatever hole we had come from was gone. Vete, who was in front of us, turned around and the girl quickly released my hand.

"I'll go find the group," he said.

I nodded my head and said, "we'll stay in the sky."

He looked at me, then the girl and then disappeared. My first attempt at talking to the girls, when Vete and I first met them, ended in failure, but if at first you do not succeed … I faced her, slowly extended my wings up at an angle and folded them behind me slightly at an angle to try to look impressive.

"So," I began, "what's your name?"

An eternity passed between us as she stared into my hood. I could almost swear she was staring into my eyes. Her hazel eyes had a story behind them, I could tell. Something horrible made her and her sisters refuse to talk. What was their story? What was her story? She finally opened her mouth.

"I found the desert," said Vete behind me.

Her mouth shut just as quickly as I jumped. The look in her eyes said Vete had arrived too soon.

113

I faced Vete and said, "alright. Let's go." He gave me another long look. "What?" I asked.

"We already passed the test in the cave," he said, "we don't have to go back. Why not just explore?"

He was going to say something else, but I spoke first. "Fine with me! There's just the sea and mountain left, ain't it? let's go!"

There was a soft, short sound behind me. It was almost a whisper, almost a giggle. I turned my head towards her. I did not think Vete heard, but I did.

I walked to her and said, "I heard that," as softly as I could as I passed her.

"What's that way?" I asked aloud.

"The sea. The desert is that way." I assumed the last part he said to the girl.

"Well, the sea it is."

Chapter 5

When I lived in Florida, the beach was a twenty minute drive away. One summer my cousin and I had found young jellyfish and buried them in the sand. The blue sea was clearer the closer to the shore I was. The waves were perfect. Sea shells could be found every foot or two. I had also been to a few aquariums before, one of which had a tunnel with a glass ceiling and glass walls. The combination of those two descriptions was what we found when we arrived at the other edge of the forest. It was a vast, clear blue sea. We could see many creatures in the same water as if salt water and fresh water coexisted in one place. Even more amazing was the fish swimming near the huge shark in the water as if it would not eat them at any moment. I saw two humpback whales and fish with various colors and shapes. I thought I saw a humongous egg in the water surrounded by much smaller pink ones, but as they floated closer to the surface I began to see the strings. They were jellyfish.

"Let's pass the salvation test," said Vete, breaking my trance. He was pointing to a large, clear tube which came out of the sea onto the beach floor.

"Like an aquarium," I said.

We flew down to the tube and the three of us were as giddy as little kids in a candy store. We may not have said it, but we were all excited to take this tour of the sea. The girl had a huge grin on her face and her eyes lit up. Vete's face was the same and mine was, too. The tube led below the surface, showing the wonders of this heavenly sea, but after a while of walking downhill we reached a point where darkness filled the water. Up until then we had seen many colorful fish and clear water, but right in front of us was darkness across the sea. I could not even see the tube in front of us, but we kept walking anyway.

"So this must be where the test begins," I said.

Vete nodded his head. A few feet into darkness the downward slope became much steeper. Vete slipped on something and slid down. I slipped immediately after him and the girl slipped immediately after me. As I said before, at this point in my life, I was not fond of roller coasters because of the drops. I did not like the feeling of being strapped down to something plummeting to the ground not under my control while I could not breathe and my stomach was wanting to jump out of my mouth. Oddly enough, on my second time on the same ride I would be completely fine with the drops. This drop, unfortunately, was the former experience. The slide ended with the girl's two hands on my large wings and my face smothered in Vete's.

I folded my large wings into my back and extended my smaller wings to the girl, who took them in her hands, and said to Vete, "Oo, e er een ow eye ay." The feathers left my face. "Thanks," I said.

My voice echoed a bit in the tube. I could feel the girl's hands begin to gently glide across my lower wings. I was about to stand up, but stopped when I heard a thud.

"We have to crawl," said Vete.

"So we can't walk, huh?"

"Here, grab my wing and stay together."

"Good idea. This would be the part in the movie where some monster comes outa nowhere or the tunnel floods."

"Let's not speak certain things into exis-tence, Tekon."

"Hey man, I'm just sayin'. If you expect these things, you won't be surprised when they happen. How are we supposed to pass this test anyway? I mean, Hunter never tells us what to do or how to pass. Well, except for the city where we had to find him, but what's that got to do with righteousness? And he didn't tell us anything about how to pass the desert test."

"I have a theory. Watch out, we're going steeper again. I think that a situation like you described is coming up at some point, and we should trust in God to be our salvation."

"That's a good idea, but things seem to work a bit differently here than on Earth. I think salvation might be a little different, too. We're in spiritual bodies right now, right? So what's there to be saved from? Death? We can't die as CBA's, can we?"

"I don't see why we can't. How blessed and holy are those who participate in the first resurrection: on such the second death hath no power."

"The first resurrection being referred to there is the rapture though. Those who are raptured won't die or die again if they were already dead."

"Has the rapture happened yet?"

"No."

"Then we can die."

A large, white oval appeared to our right. We stopped crawling and starred like deer into headlights. The light came closer slowly, but surely. By the time I thought of what the light could be, Vete was already acting. It all happened in slow motion. I could feel the tug of Vete's wing as he tried to quickly pull us to safety. The tube cracked and shattered. Water filled the space and pounded my face as smaller lights appeared, making a trail from the oval to the teeth. I lost my grip on Vete's wing and felt the girl's hand slip off of mine. I could not think. I knew I had to, but I could not. There was no light except for what was produced by the giant angler fish whose teeth seemed to continue to grow. I kept my mouth shut, though I wanted to scream. Vete had pulled us just in time to avoid the initial bite. The fish turned its head towards me and my heart almost broke my chest. I needed oxygen. I needed to breathe, but to breathe was to die. A white figure swam towards the creature. It must have been Vete. The fish noticed him and quickly swam towards him, teeth ready to tear him to shreds. My mind went a thousand miles an hour. What was Vete doing!? Did he want to die!?

'Trust in God, Tekon,' the soft, gentle voice echoed inside my head.

I was nearing my limit on holding my breath. Vete stopped and turned to me. As the teeth were closing in, he pointed up and spread out his wings. The teeth closed and he was gone.

'Tekon,' echoed the voice, 'remember this.'

I let out what little air I held in my lungs and tried to hold my breath, still.

'Whosoever shall seek to save his life shall lose it;' the voice continued.

I could not keep my mouth closed any longer. Water rushed into my lungs and burned. I panicked.

'And whosoever shall lose his life shall preserve it,' finished the voice.

My throat burned and I felt like I was choking on a long rope which could not come out of my throat. I felt myself become heavy. In my mind I screamed for Jesus. There was a bright light, the oval, and then teeth. Time went in slow motion again, but much slower than the previous. I saw a white feather in the teeth. It brought me back to a memory of a time where I was sitting at the funeral of some family member whom I did not know. Everyone was dressed in black, the casket open. People said good things about her. My step-dad, who was then just a friend, was invited to the funeral as well and asked to sing and play. He did not know a thing about the dead woman, but when it was his turn in the ceremony, he said if she was ever asked why she would be happy in bad times she would sing this hymn: I sing, because I'm happy, I sing because I'm free, for His eye is on the sparrow, and I know He watches me. The teeth closed in and I closed my eyes, knowing God would take care of me.

I cannot fully explain what happened next because I do not fully understand it myself.

'I'm so proud of you, Tekon,' the soft, gentle voice echoed inside my head.

Opening my eyes again was like waking up from another bad dream. Scared moments before, I was now surrounded by clear water, dolphins, jellyfish of various colors, a blue fish with red stripes, a stingray and many other types of aquatic life. I would have held my breath were I not already breathing. Wait, I was breathing underwater! A sea tortuous swam by with Vete sitting on top with his legs crossed.

He looked at me and said, "she'll be here soon."

I heard his voice as if he were speaking in air and not water. He flapped his wings slowly back and forth as if to propel him and his tortuous.

"How'd you know you wouldn't die?" I asked.

Without looking back, he said, "I didn't."

"His eye is on the sparrow," I mumbled.

There was a tap on my shoulder. I smiled and turned to face the girl. She seemed alright. She did not seem to be shaken up too bad.

"You alright?" I asked.

She smiled and nodded her head. Her hair was beautiful floating in the water. A pink blob with strings bobbed up to her side. She petted it and I could almost swear it cuddled up to her. The tentacles slowly crept up to her arm.

"Hey!" I said and reached for the blob, but Vete's hand grabbed my arm.

"Wait," he said.

The tentacles wrapped around her arm, but she did not cringe or jerk as if in pain. She instead smiled.

"The creatures in the clear water are harmless," said Vete as he let go of my arm, "I pet a shark earlier. Also, I think there is more to every part of the training room than just testing our armor. For this sea, we also get a pet it seems, but I think there's more to it than just a pet."

"So then in the dark the sea creatures must be violent. Okay. So if you have a turtle and she has a jellyfish, then what do I have?"

"That." Vete pointed to something behind me.

I turned to see a shark and jumped. It was a great white. I had hoped for an octopus or mantis shrimp, but a shark was nothing to scoff at. My video-game mindset kicked in and I had a simulated battle between my shark, Vete's turtle and the girl's jellyfish. My shark could rip the turtle's head off easily. Biting jellyfish could have serious consequences, but I was pretty sure sharks also ate jellyfish. Sea turtles ate jellyfish as well. Although a big enough jellyfish might sting an unsuspecting shark to death. I should also be wary of octopi. I petted the shark. It had rough skin like sand paper.

"Well howdy there."

We were gone too long. Hunter was above us, horizontally facing us, with his arms folded. The girl became horizontal, facing Hunter, and hid the jellyfish behind her back. Vete stood on his tortoise.

"So what'd y'all go galavantin' off fer this time?" Hunter did not look happy.

"We were exploring and passing the tests," said Vete.

"An' you think that's okay? You think that's fine? Stealin' water from the group, leavin' yer teammates behin' so you can go off an' do yer own thang?"

"No, sir," I said.

"I oughta make y'all go back to the city for a night'er two. But lucky fer you the CIC says it's okay fer y'all to go on ahead. But this is not over, gentlemen. Hope here is to go on witcha in case you cain't tell left from yer momma, but she is not to proceed with y'all's next trainin', is that understood?"

"Yes, sir," I said.

"Vete, why cain'tchu just stay with the class instead a jumpin' ahead and tryin' ta finish first? There ain't no reward for gettin' first. The first shall be last and the last shall be first. Tekon, why cain'tchu make yer own decisions and not just folla Vete wherever he goes? Hope, don't get caught up in these boys' foolishness, ya hear? Now I got a book fer you two chosens. The CIC figured since you two like ta move on ahead you might as well get a head start on yer readin'."

I looked past him and saw the others standing on the shore. Hunter walked past us and stopped just beyond the darkness. He turned to us and in his hands were two small books. He let them go and they floated up to Vete and I. The books were hardback and tan. There was a grey rectangle on the cover. In the rectangle was the title in white which read

'Chosen Prayer' in an arch across the top of the rectangle. Under the title was a man in a white robe with blue outlines. He had six wings. The top two covered his face. The bottom two covered his feet and the middle two were spread out with his arms.

"That book," continued Hunter, "will teach ya everythan' you need to know. Yer sea animals will lead you through the darkness be-hin' me to the mountains. Once yer out the wa-ter yer on yer own."

The shark nudged my side and I petted it after I put the book in one of my pant pock-ets.

Mounting the shark was an odd experi-ence, but I decided to stand with my feet on either side of the dorsal fin and said, "Jesus wept." I pressed the button and bubbles rose from my sword. "Alright," I said, "let's ride."

Vete and the girl were already in the darkness. Hunter did not look pleased at my knowing how to draw out my sword.

"Vete taught me and I taught everyone else," I said as I passed him on my shark.

Riding the shark was interesting. The shark's sways were long and smooth. For such a ferocious beast, it swam gracefully. Once in the darkness, I could not even see the white x on my weapon. It was a little terrifying at first, but I found comfort in my beast's gentle sways. It was my third time in complete darkness and I was getting used to it. For a third time, I saw a circle of light. As I got closer I saw it was actually a pillar of light. The shark swam to it and stopped with me directly in the light. I stretched my wings and flapped. The light grew brighter as I swam higher. Once I saw the edge of the water, I decided to come out looking cool. With another flap of my wings I jumped out of the water and stopped in midair with my wings spread out and my sword slanted down to my right.

"Nice pose," said Vete behind me.

I jumped. "Dude," I said, "did you at least see me come out?"

"Yes, I did."

I descended to the cave floor, but did not let my feet touch the ground. The light source came from light green crystals which grew in similar fashion to stalactites and stalagmites, but the light was clear rather than tinted green. There were also dark blue crystals as well. Some crystals were larger than Vete and I.

"Where's Hope?" I asked.

Her name sounded foreign to my lips. Vete walked while I hovered.

"I think she went exploring," he said.

I decided to make us souvenirs, so I brought out my weapon and started hacking away at large crystals while Vete read the book we were just given. I hacked and slashed for a while before Hope came into view. She stood by me as I sat with a rough crystal in hand, trimming it by scraping it against my sword.

"I'm making souvenirs," I said, "one green and one blue for each of us."

She nodded her head and walked off. It took me a while, but eventually I managed to get the crystals down to the size of a club which could fit in our hands. They were the length of my palm to my elbow and two square inches thick. Unfortunately, none of my pant pockets were deep enough to hold the crystals. I gave Vete and Hope their crystals and decided to just hold mine in both hands. Vete stuffed his in his robe somewhere. I was unaware he had any pockets. Hope apparently had large pockets as well in her outfit.

"So y'all ready to go?" I asked.

They both nodded. Hope led us to the only dark tunnel, because it had no crystals, and took out her green crystal. I still could not see where her pocket line was so it was as if she pulled the crystal out of thin air. Once we stepped in the dark tunnel, our crystals began to shine in their natural color and so there was a mixture of blue and green light in the cave.

"So Vete," I began, "what are we supposed to do here again? Test our shields of faith?"

"Yes our shields will be tested," he answered, "by various situations that seem impossible to block. For example.."

He pointed in the direction we were headed. There was nothing there at first, but the sound of rushing water which grew louder.

"My turn," he said.

He stepped in front of me and I looked ahead of him to see green water rushing toward us, filling the entire cave. I put both of my crystals in one hand, expecting Hope to grab the other. I did not expect her to squeeze the life out of it.

"Stay close to me," he yelled over the noise.

We huddled close to him. While the green water rushed towards us, Vete remained calm and in control, but my heart was using my chest as a drum set. The water came and I closed my eyes, but I remained dry. I opened my eyes again and saw the water rushing around us as if we were in a sphere of protection. Vete turned around and it was as if the water was coming from his back at all angles.

"Just have faith," he yelled over the noise, "that your shield will protect you."

The water died down and I watched the remnants trickle from the invisible dome we were in. Hope released my hand and I took the lead. We walked for a while with Vete in the rear while I experimented with the angles at which I could bend my wings. I had just stretched out all my wings to either side when I saw a bright orange light far off in the distance.

"Here it comes," I said.

The fire did not fill the cave like the water did. It came in a long column aimed right at the x on my chest. I had envisioned turning around, facing Hope and having whatever came reflect off my shield looking like the water did with Vete. What actually happened was something much different. I got nervous thinking about them both watching me and became self conscious of how I would look. How would my wings look? Would my shield also protect me from the force of the fire, or just the burn? Would my wings and back of my cloak get burned since my shield was on my back? Intense heat blasted me out of my thoughts and I quickly turned around just in time to avoid chest burn. The momentum of the fire knocked me into Hope and I held her as we were pushed through the air towards Vete. My back burned as if a hot iron had been pressed to it and the steam button also pressed. I screamed in pain briefly, but once I saw Vete I remembered to have faith. My back began to recover and we slowed to a stop in midair in front of Vete while I was still holding on to Hope. Hope's arms were wrapped around me. Did she wrap them when I first grabbed her or once we stopped? I could not tell.

I stayed in the air with Hope until my shield completely cooled down. Vete was observing his two crystals. Once I let Hope stand on the ground, blue and green crystals appeared in the tunnel as if they were always there to begin with, but this time the light was green rather than white. Vete walked past me and gave me a look.

"What?" I asked.

"You don't know her," he said softly.

"Dude," I said.

I hovered behind him and Hope walked beside me. I swung my crystals around as we went.

"So next is the sword, right?" I asked.

"We've already mastered drawing our swords," said Vete, "so I don't think we'll be testing them. We've used them plenty of times already."

"True. So then we're off to the final test, huh?"

"Yes."

At the end of the tunnel I almost expected to see Hunter, but instead I saw the sea again.

"Dude!" I yelled. I flew out to the water and started walking on it. Actually I was flying low enough to step on the water. It reminded me of Peter from the Bible, but Peter never flew.

"Tekon!" I heard Vete yell.

He was standing on a path alongside the mountain. In front of him was a caucasian man with short black hair wearing a white blazer decorated with black musical notes. He had a solid black tie in an Eldridge knot with a white treble clef pin on it. He also wore solid black pants and black shoes with white tips. I flew to them and Hope stood beside me. The man had piercing blue eyes.

"What's going on?" I asked.

"What's going on?" The man mimicked my voice exactly.

"Dude!" I said, "did you just...!? Do it again!"

"Someone else, please," he said in my voice again.

"Are you here to test our abilities?" asked Vete.

"Yes," he answered in Vete's voice, "the girl may go now."

Hope nodded her head and walked back down to the caves.

"You know," said the man in Vete's voice, "you weren't supposed to take the crystals yet." He crossed his arms. "Hunter was right. You two like to rush things. You've ditched your team twice, used your first wishes, completed two tests ahead of your team without permission, learned to fly before the others and how to make your weapons materialize."

"How do you know about the wishes?" I asked.

"Your spiritual potency, for one," he said in my voice, "and because the CIC has been watching you."

"Then are you the voice we've been hearing in the desert and the forest and the city?" asked Vete.

"What voice?" he asked in my voice.

"The voice that's been making us use our wishes," I said.

He shook his head. "I'm sorry," he said in Vete's voice, "but I don't know what you're talking about, cherub junior. The CIC has many responsibilities and few staff, but we've seen Vete using angelic speed in the city and we saw what happened in the church. Also, spiritual potency changes once a wish has been used. That's how we know you've used your first wish, Vete. Now there's no more time for chit chat. I'm running on a tight schedule. I have a symphony to orchestrate in two hours, a choir to teach and a piano recital afterwards, and I don't mean our time. I mean Earth time, mind you."

"Talk in your own voice, please," said Vete, "and what's your name?"

"I don't have my own voice," he said in mine.

"Dude," I said, "you don't have your own voice?"

"No," he remained in mine, "and my name is Treble."

"Oh," I said, "so what's the CIC? What's spiritual potency and how is it measured?"

"No no no," said Treble in my voice, "no time for that now. Let's begin."

We began our lesson by saying a prayer.

I was in a bed. My father stood beside me.

"Good morning, son," he said.

"Good morning, Dad," I yawned.

"You feeling alright?"

"A little. I feel tired though."

"Well there's breakfast in the kitchen. The doctor said you needed to get a few days of rest and let it all sink in. If you need anything, let me know."

"Yes, sir."

Let it all sink in.

Whenever I suffered a loss of someone and the loss was deep enough or severe enough to cause my days to be filled with depression, I would try to sleep my days away. I did this to escape reality and live in my dreams where the world was much better and things were happy and exciting. In my dreams, there was always adventure, and whomever I had just lost would be there. We would be together, happy. Once I woke up, my mind would realize I was back in reality and there was no escaping. I would wake up in disappointment. What happened did actually happen. This was reality. My dreams were nothing more than fantasies. The person was gone. I needed to move on, but how could I? Surely if I had done things better, or said something different, the person would still be in my life. Usually this thinking applied to girls I had liked who were no longer a part of my love life, but today this applied to a friend whom I was unable to protect. I replayed the scene in my head, imagining things I could have done or said differently. Perhaps if I had done those things Reagan would still be here. If I had told her I had some cash on me I could have given her, she would not have gone in the bank at all. If I had thought of a plan rather than just reacting to the situation I could have found a better way to get the gun from the man and Reagan would still be here. The sadness struck my heart and I began to cry. I buried my face in the white pillow and cried as quietly as I could. I could tell I was in a hotel, but I did not bother to observe my surroundings. It did not matter. What mattered was Reagan was gone and every morning I would wake up from my dreams and deal with the depression of reality. I did not know how long it took before I cried myself to sleep.

"Welcome back," said Treble in my father's voice.

Vete looked at me.

"My father," I said to Vete. "Were you there?" I asked Treble.

"I was at first, but switched to viewing Vete's Prayer Life shortly after. Now let's begin."

Vete's fight was first and ended in a flash. I never even saw him take out his sword. One moment he was standing in front of Treble and the next he was behind him.

"You pass," said Treble in Professor's voice. Then he switched to David's voice and said, "well, I must be going now. Hunter will be administering your final test, Tekon. Apparently you upset him quite a bit in the city. As an employee of the CIC I wouldn't advise upsetting him. Good day you two." He walked down into the caves.

"What'd you do?" asked Vete.

"I may or may not have implied that Hunter lied," I said sheepishly.

Vete raised an eyebrow. "You called an angel a liar?"

"No! I asked if there was the possibility that he could, since he was knockin' folks out in his sleep, and we're not supposed to sleep in heaven, but since this ain't heaven and he can sleep, he can lie, too cain't he?"

"I understand your theory and I agree with you, but you shouldn't call him out on that. They're the ones with all the power here and we don't even know all there is to know about this place or about being a Class B Angel."

"True. True. Oh well. If all angels are as fast as or faster than you then I'm done, so we'll see."

I flew over the water and looked at the sea creatures below.

'You will become a great Class B Angel, Tekon,' echoed the soft, gentle voice inside my head. I had almost forgotten about the voice.

"You ready?"

I did not forget this voice. I turned around and Hunter swung his gunblade down at me. I blocked with the crystals in an x formation.

"Dude!" I said.

"Time to test yer metal."

A kick to my gut sent me flying to the mountain. Right when I remembered my shield of faith, I hit the ground. I did not have time to think about what would have happened had I not remembered my shield because Hunter's gunblade was swinging down at me. I blocked again. When he lifted his weapon to strike again I rolled to the side. When he struck again I hit his sword to the side. I got up and swung the other crystal at him, but he disappeared. I instinctively thought of my shield, but wondered if I could take a kick to the back since the fire burned earlier. My lack of faith in my shield cost me pain in my kidneys followed by a stinging pain on the entire front side of my body as if I was slammed into a concrete wall. Out of old Earthly habits I held my breath, swam up to the water's surface and gasped for air. Hunter hovered above with his gunblade aimed at me. Past him I saw Vete in the distance holding the crystals I had dropped.

"Come on, now," said Hunter, "where's all that power you had before?"

"Dude," I said, slowly rising from the water, "Jesus wept."

I threw the laser sword hilt in the air, jumped out of the water, spun around as the hilt came back down and pressed the button while my wings extended. Hunter laughed and my self consciousness returned.

Laughing, he asked, "what's that s'posed to be?"

I lunged at him, but my blade was blocked by his and he still laughed. "You been watchin' too many cartoons," he said.

I remained silent and assaulted him with a barrage of slashes, kicks and punches. He blocked every single attack with his gunblade.

"This all you got?" he asked.

I swung my sword at him, but he reached forward and grabbed my sword-holding wrist with one hand and sent an uppercut to my stomach which knocked the wind out of me and lifted me higher in the air.

As I was laying on his fist, he leaned in and said, "your armor's weak." I watched my wings hang from either side. "When you go have yer next Prayer Life," he continued, "work on righteous living."

His fist opened and closed, this time with a bit of my coat inside. I looked up in time to see the mountain zooming at me. I flipped forward and tried to fly in the opposite direction as fast as I could, which slowed me down enough to land on the mountain wall without pain. I did not expect him to throw me. I noticed Vete beside me. How did he pass this test? I heard a gunshot and ducked in time to avoid a bullet where my head just was.

"Dude aims for head shots," I said to myself, "and I'm the zombie. Great."

I stabbed the mountain with my sword, turned it and pulled it out. Wind blew at me from every direction and something threw me off the mountain wall. I was blown around the mountain back into the tunnel I had emerged from earlier. When the winds died down I was in front of a green laser shield. The shield lowered and I could see Terminator's confused face.

"Tekon?" he asked, almost in disbelief.

"Practicing for your faith test, huh?" I asked.

Larry was behind him and Hope was with her sisters. When she saw me she smiled, tucked her hair behind her ear and waved.

I waved and said, "hey Ho-"

Hunter appeared and kicked me in the gut, which cut off my sentence at a very inconvenient time and sent me through the cave walls to the sea again. Thank the Lord I had thought of my shield the moment Hunter appeared. After I stopped bouncing on the water's surface like a skipped stone, I slid a few feet before I finally stopped and stood on the water. I pointed my sword at the new tunnel in the mountain and noticed the white glowing x on my right glove. The last time the x was lit I struck Hunter with a lot of force behind it, but I also got teleported to the pocket realm with Vadallat who wanted to use me as a conduit for something. I heard a gunshot and raised my weapon defensively. Something hit my sword and splashed in the water a few feet away. Hunter appeared in front of me and I immediately slashed as if on instinct. He blocked again with his gunblade, but my swing pushed him down into the water with a big splash while his posture remained unchanged. I continued to push down and we went deeper into the water. I heard Hunter whistle as we went. As we went down I noticed he was looking at the white x on the back of my hand. He reached for his cap and took it off. It floated to my face and I tried to reach for it, but pain struck my right arm, then my right leg, then my left thigh, then my stomach, then my chest and left arm. I was in a peculiar pain and could not move. The hat was removed from my face and placed back on Hunter's head. He tipped his hat to me as I sank towards the dark portion of the sea. My heart began to race.

'Don't be afraid, Tekon,' the soft, gentle voice echoed inside my head, 'trust in God.'

She was right, I thought, I needed to trust in God. He did not bring me this far to leave me. He may not come when I want Him, but He will be there right on time. He is an on time God. Yes He is.

Just as I passed into the darkness, something pushed me up. When I was back in the light I was staring at a shark. I was frightened at first, but then I remembered it to be the shark from before. My limbs began to tingle as if my foot was asleep and I was waking it up again. I turned around on the shark and launched myself off of it. Hunter was just above the water's surface. He looked down at me just before I flew out of the water and struck him. He blocked again, but this time I sent him flying and I flew after him. When I caught up to him, before he could recover, I slashed again. He managed to block, but he was sent flying to the mountain. He backflipped in midair and landed on his feet. I flew at him and he blocked my next slash with no problem. I looked at my glove and the x was no longer glowing. He looked as well.

"Fight's over, Tekon," he said, "congratulations. Yer now an official Class B Angel."

Part 2

Chapter 6

"Now would be a good time for a Prayer Life." Vete was standing on the ledge of a cliff looking at a city below. The moon and stars were shining bright as if there were glitter frozen in the space around him. "Once we go in there," he continued, "we're going to need you at your best."

"Yeah. I'll get right on that." I bowed my head, looked down at the city below and closed my eyes. "Dear God our heavenly Father..."

I rose from my seat, left a two dollar tip for my one dollar drink and headed out the door. The city was bustling with people doing their last minute shopping as the sun set. I used to call this real life, being in my human body, but I spent little time in it now. Now my time spent in my CB (Class B) body was real life. As I walked along the sidewalk, memories of what my body was doing without me slowly began to flow. How long had it been since I had last been in my human body? A month per-haps? A memory of a show presented itself to me. It was a comedy. The main character had just done something funny.

I walked downhill to a nearby church along the road. The entire front doors were glass. Another layer of glass doors sat behind them. As I figured, the front doors were locked, so I walked to the back side of the church where the prayer room was. I sat with my back to the wall and waited for the memories to end. It had been two years since Reagan's abduction. Two years since the nightmares began. Two years since guilt and depression became my closest friends. I still had not faced her parents, though I had received countless letters from them telling me they loved me and were thankful I tried to save her and was still trying. I left my human body to escape all of this. I remembered the nightmares, the depression, the guilt, but I did not feel them. The memories finally stopped.

I looked at the starry sky and said, "dear God our heavenly Father..."

"You ready?" asked Vete. He was crouched beside me with his back to the city.

"Yeah," I said.

"Alright guys," said Vete as he stood, "overview. My team's going to take the west side and fan out. Tekon's team will take the east side. If our target's spotted, no one is to do anything until either I or Tekon give the okay. There will be no mishaps this time."

This time. This was the fifth rescue mission where we had tried to rescue Reagan. Each time, we came close, but something unexpected always happened.

"Tekon," said Vete.

"Yeah?"

"We're going to save her this time."

He always said this, to which I always replied, "Lord-willing."

Vete and his team of CB's flew past me. I turned to my team. They all wore a black coat with a white x across the chest, but all their hoods were down. Terminator, Hope and Larry had volunteered to be on my team when they finished their initial CB training. They had been with me the longest. The other two members of my team were newly recruited CB's. It was their first mission. I back-stepped to the edge of the cliff and leaned back. My team flew after me. Something black struck my face as I fell. I stopped and looked around.

"Sir!" came a voice from above.

I looked up to see my team fighting Sin. Sin were small, black monkeys with leathery wings, sharp claws and sharper fangs. There were just a few of them, but they were nimble, agile. It was hard to see them in the night sky, but I could tell where they were by their annoy-ing, loud, high pitched screeches.

One flew at me. It seemed about three feet long. I slid my crystals from either sleeve and struck it across its face. It let out a painful yelp, followed shortly by an angry screech. Two more flew to its aid, then all three rushed me, claws extended. I dodged the first and struck the other two with both crystals, but the tail from the first Sin wrapped around my neck. I hit the Sin with both of my large wings. It let out a yelp and its grip loosened. The other two were back and I leaned backwards just in time to miss a claw as one Sin flew in front of my face. The other came directly to me, screeching loudly. I ducked and put a crystal above my head, striking the Sin just as it was over my head.

"Terminator! Time!" I yelled.

"We got ten minutes!" he yelled back.

Ten minutes.

Ten minutes.

Ten minutes.

"Tekon!" a girl yelled.

A Sin jumped in my face. All I saw were its face and fangs.

I woke up. I was in my hotel room in Babel Hotel. The alarm clock kept repeating "ten minutes." I quickly reached over and turned off the alarm.

'How are you this morning, Tekon?' the gentle voice echoed softly inside my head.

I sat up in my bed. Outside the window I could see the sun begin to rise. I watched the magnificent flash of light erase all traces of the previous night's horrors. My coat was draped over the counter in the kitchen. The dream. I had dreamt the same dream five times in a month. I had nine minutes to report to the bottom of the hotel. I made a bowl of cereal and was about to take the first bite when there was a knock on the door. I put the spoon down in the bowl and looked trough the peephole. It was Vete. It was always Vete. Usually, while I ate whatever breakfast I had, he would eat some fruit. I let him in. He had a cluster of grapes.

"You know," said Vete, standing by the kitchen counter after he ate the last grape, "pretty soon we'll graduate as chosens and get our first missions."

"Yeah, I know. It's been a while since they taught us about it, though. We get to choose our missions, right?"

"We get assigned missions for a while until we get used to them. Then we'll be able to choose our own team or solo missions."

"Oh yeah, we're supposed to work with other angels and learn the tricks of the trade until we can be successful guardian angels, right? Then we can orchestrate our own missions."

"Correct."

"Then once all the chosens are proficient in their abilities and leadership, it'll be us orchestrating the regulars as guardian angels while we lead and perform other tasks, right?"

"That's what they tell us."

"Yeah. And at some point before all this the angels are supposed to pass on the ability to slay Sin and even demons, which will finalize our replacing them. ... Am I missing anything?"

"No, you got it all. You'll pass the final exams. Don't worry."

"Test taking is not my strongest point, man."

"Well you've done good so far. Let's go."

I had done good so far because I had always been paired with Vete who caught on to things very quickly. For the past month, after the final armor test on the mountain, Vete and I were to report to the city, which I found out was called Anima Nex Vita. There we met other chosens and were going to be given special training by David and Professor. We learned many things about being a Class B Angel and what Sin were and how to fight them and how to fight demons should we ever come across them. I did not pay much attention during the lessons because my mind was always focussed on when I would get to search for Reagan and how I would find her. We did most assessments in teams, which was how I made passing scores. On the solo exams I did not do so well. The final exam was to be a solo exam.

The bottom of the hotel could not be seen from the lobby. There were platforms jutting inward from the spiral walkway which were extensions of each section of the building, except for the hotel lobby. People could spend their entire lives inside Babel Hotel without ever leaving. There was a shopping section, an education section, an agricultural section and even a religious section, just to name a few. Each section housed everything having to do with its section. For example, the religious section had a temple for every organized religion known to man and every denomination of the religion. Needless to say, each section of the hotel was massive. From what I understood, the citizens, or Citizen Souls as we called them, of Anima Nex Vita got around from section to section via a very complex system of tunnels which led to literally every establishment inside Babel Hotel. CBA's were not allowed in the traveling tunnels. If we wanted to go somewhere, we had to go in through the spiral walkway entrance. Flying was much faster than walking and even running, so it was not a big issue to me.

     Vete and I flew down to the bottom, passing each of the many sections along the way. People in the religious section were saying morning prayers for the families of those who lost loved ones during the previous night. At the bottom of the spiral stood hundreds of winged Class B Angels. Some wings were blue, pink, yellow or green, but most were white and feathered. I had gotten to know the names of a few of them over the month. We stood there at the bottom and waited for our instructors, David and Professor, but they did not show. This was nothing new. They had not shown up on time before to test our patience and our sandals of peace. We waited and conversed with other chosens for almost two hours before everyone began to worry.

"Well, not that this ain't fun," I said, "but if they ain't comin' I'd rather go explore some more."

I had been exploring different sections with Vete every day after training.

"Sounds good to me," said Vete, "we can be back in a flash when they get here."

Vete was the other reason I did not mind being denied access to the traveling tunnels. Vete could get me anywhere in the blink of an eye.

"Alright. Let's do the storage tunnels to-day. The only tunnels we're not denied access to in here."

At the very bottom of the hotel where we were there were storage tunnels which were hardly ever used. We left the huddle of worried feathers and headed for a tunnel. There were tunnel entrances along the walls of the bottom floor with golden plaques as labels above each entrance, but the letters were worn out on each of them. We picked the first entrance we saw and started walking. There was a light switch along the tunnel wall near the entrance, but it did not work. I would have pulled out a crystal for lighting, but outside of the faith caves the green crystals only lit when Sin were around and the blue when demons were around. Also I had left my crystals in my room. Light from the bottom floor lit the tunnel dimly all the way to the first turn. After the first turn, the ground was barely lit, but my eyes adjusted as we went on.

We kept walking down the tunnel past a few crates until we heard a voice around the next corner. There was a crate along the wall so Vete and I crouched behind it.

"Stole the girl, you say!?" said a high pitch male voice. The voice was very familiar to me.

"She has a certain power," said another man's voice, "that will help us get the Grail."

Hysterical laughter followed. I remembered the voice. The voice from the forest and desert where Vete and I used our first wishes. The voice in Anima Nex Vita when I was with Hope. I focused on breathing as quietly as I could and stepped out from behind the crate.

"Do you really think that girl's power will help you get the Grail?" asked the familiar voice with a chuckle.

Vete grabbed my shoulder. I looked at him. He was wide-eyed and shook his head fiercely.

"Oh you demons crack me up!" said the familiar voice.

I silently stepped forward.

The demon scoffed and said, "her spiritual senses are the highest of any demi-angel."

Another heart-pounding step.

"And only demi-angels can sense the Grail," said the demon.

Another step. I could feel my body shaking. I had to take slow, deep, silent breaths.

"Yesyesyes and you need the Grail to start your war, stick it to the man, destroy heaven, blah blah blah," said the voice.

I was at the edge of the corner now. The two voices were just on the other side. I put my back to the wall. With my dark outfit I could probably peek my head past the edge and still not be seen.

"Just remember your end of the deal," continued the voice.

I could do it. I could peek my head over and see who was there. I could finally put a face to the voice.

"Don't worry about that," said the demon, "just be ready when Greed comes."

I could do it. So why not right then and there? There was no way I could be seen. Do it. Just do it.

"Oh, Greed wants little ole me!? I feel so special!"

"Can you be serious for five minutes?"

"Sorry, sir."

"Now what about the boy?"

Hysterical laughter. Why could I not do this? They were not expecting anyone else to be there. There was no reason to. They would not even see me.

"Smart as a cherub, that boy. Figured out my trap in a jiffy. Or is that a human food?"

"Has he used his first two wishes?"

"He's used his first wish, but he does have a new power now."

"I thought the first wish could only be used to benefit someone else more than the caster?"

"Well you see, those two are insepara-ble. My forest trap would've produced a fine waste of a wish were it not for the smart one wanting angelic speed rather than simply get-ting out of the trap. Then when it came his turn to use a wish, instead of escaping the fire he wished for the other one's sword to be a get-out-of-jail-free card."

"You fool. Now the Chronos Scindo can't be used. And I won't be the one to tell that to Wrath."

"Oh you simpleton. The Chronos Scindo can still be used. I have other traps to use on boy wonder."

"You better, or.."

There was a pause. I felt Vete grab and pull me back. Just as Vete pulled me away, I caught a glimpse of someone's head begin to peek around the corner. Quicker than a flash, we were in the middle of the crowd of chosens.

"Vete," I said, heart racing.

"I know," he replied.

"That voice."

"I know."

"The girl."

"It's possible."

"The Grail? The Holy Grail?"

"We'll have to find out about that."

"Sorry I'm late chosens," Professor's voice was heard over the talk of the crowd.

The crowd hushed as we all faced the direction of the voice.

"Vete," I said.

"I know," he replied.

"Since I'm late today," said Professor, "use today as a practice for your combat prayers, alright?"

The way Class B Angels were to fight was through prayer. Any fight was known as a prayer battle since we were prayer warriors. We started the battle by bringing out the word (our swords) by praying the word (quoting scripture to summon our swords). Once the battle was started, there were certain powers God allowed Class B Angels to have which we could use to fight with. For chosens they were called combat prayers and were split into three classes: battle, support and prophetic. Battle prayers could hurt the foe. Support prayers were sub-classified by healing prayers or defensive prayers. Prophetic prayers were as the name implied. We were allotted three prayers. Each prayer required the CBA to be at a certain spiritual potency level before it could be used. Spiritual potency was increased by the way we lived our prayer lives, but only God could measure our spiritual potency. The prayers we chose could not be replaced. So once we chose a combat prayer, we were stuck with it. It was rumored the most powerful combat prayers were ones directly quoted from scripture, but the most creative ones were original. Because the regular CBA's way of fighting was different than how chosens fought, the CIC made a rule stating our prayers must be specific if we wanted God to answer them with a "yes" when we battled. At the end of any battle, when we let our swords vanish, we had to say, "in Jesus' name, amen." Saying so signified the end of the prayer; the end of the battle.

Having spent many hours dreaming of my dream character long ago, I was a bit saddened I could only have three extra powers. My dream character had quite a few, but if one of my prayers was to summon my dream character then I would be happy. On the day we learned about combat prayers I asked Professor about it.

I explained to him my dream character, which wore a dark coat like me, but without the bottom bent out. He also wore a hood in which you could not see his face. He was a ninja. On his back was an extendable golden staff and two katanas. He had two swords hidden in his sleeves. Each weapon had special tags on them which could summon a clone of him which specialized in fighting with the summoning weapon as well as summon the actual character if need be, like a limited teleportation.

He had two water jutsus. One was a sphere of water which could be used to trap something or smash through something. The other was a ring of water surrounding him which would heal injuries and protect from outside threats.

His ultimate jutsu was when the five weapons were separated from him and his clones were summoned. They would form a pentagon with him in the center and go through the five phase process. Phase one drained energy from all opponents in the pentagon. Phase two transferred the drained energy to the character, increasing his speed and strength and powered the circular metal plates on the back of his hands. When in the pentagon he fought by backhanding his opponents. Upon contact the plates would release a burst of energy, making the backhands quite powerful.

When the third phase activated, invisible barriers were raised from the pentagon and a burst of light incinerated everything except the ninja. Should the opponent(s) survive, the fourth phase was activated in which everything and everyone who made it to the fifth phase was summoned to protect the ninja and fight the foe(s). Should the opponent(s) survive one hour of the fourth phase (which would be incredible since the first and second phase remained active), the fifth phase activated and the surviving foe(s) were forever sealed inside the pentagon jutsu. The ninja then had an hour to find a safe place to rest for an entire year in a coma. However, if the ninja decided not to use the third phase, then the ninja just had to simply wait a month to use the technique again.

After explaining my dream character to Professor, he scratched his head and said, "Um, no. The CIC would find that a bit, how you say, overpowered. Even if the creator of all things decided to grant you that prayer, I'm sure the spiritual potency level would be tremendously high. Why don't you instead focus on scriptural prayers? That will also increase the strength of your sword and perhaps your shield. Or, if you're really focussed on that character, find three specific abilities you would want and use those."

So I chose to instead think strategically about my options. I decided to have a scriptural healing prayer and two battle prayers. Vete chose to have all scriptural prophetic prayers.

The chosens flew their separate ways to train. Some talked about going to the arcade in the entertainment section to practice in the virtual arena. Others talked about relaxing instead. Vete and I stayed to see where Professor would go. Once the chosens cleared out, I could see the same podium he stood behind when I first met him.

"Can I help you, boys?" asked Professor.

"Where were you, Professor?" Vete asked.

"Delayed. Are you going to train in here?"

"It's beneficial for me to train with someone who can match my speed."

The next thing I saw was the ground.

"Tekon's too easy," said Vete.

"Oh thanks man," I said sarcastically, "now get off me."

Professor sighed, scratched his head and walked towards us. The bottom of the hotel had a large dark green diamond in the center of the dark grey concrete tile floor with dark blue flower designs throughout.

"What's your plan?" I asked Vete.

I looked to him for an answer, but Professor appeared between us. He reached for me, but Vete appeared in front of me and was grabbed instead.

"Jesus wept." I swerved around Vete and slashed at Professor, but he disappeared. Vete was wide-eyed. "Dude, you alright?" I asked.

He blinked a few times and said, "don't let him touch you."

I nodded my head and said, "right." What happened when he touched Vete? I flew to the ground and yelled, "Mutatio machina!"

My voice had a slight echo to it. Mutatio machina literally meant "transform machine." It allowed me to sense and animate machines within a hundred feet of me. Below me I could sense water pipes. In response to my will, two large pipes emerged from the ground and coiled around me defensively. Vete and Professor were fighting on the ground using martial arts skills, but Vete seemed to be losing. I pointed my sword at Professor and a pipe extended to him. Just as it was about to encase him, he disappeared and reappeared in front of me. Again his ominous hand reached for me, but Vete appeared between us and deflected Professor's hand up with the back of his and I willed the second pipe to encase Professor. Vete stepped back just in time.

"Congratulations, boys," said Professor from inside the pipe, "you've managed to capture me momentarily, but boys, it was not me in the tunnel."

I looked at Vete.

"It's his power," said Vete, "just by touching you, he learns all your memories. When he grabbed me, it was as if the whole world went away and it was just him and I, and everything I could ever remember was played in front of us like a movie."

"All that when he grabbed you?" I asked.

"Yes," answered Vete.

"Boys," said Professor, "if you let me out I'd be more than happy to help you find this mystery demon and his accomplice that has troubled you in times past."

"I assume if he wanted to get out by now he could've," I said, "so might as well."

I restored the pipes to their original position and was greeted by an unearthly foul odor from the angel.

"Let me go shower, first," said Professor.

Chapter 7

The room was dim with only the setting sun to illuminate it through the window. An angel I had never seen before sat across from Vete and I. He was the first angel I had seen to have wings and he had four. Two of them covered his face. He placed both elbows on the desk separating us and held his hands up to his face.

"So tell me again just what you think you saw and heard," said the angel.

Professor was standing behind us at the door.

Vete leaned forward in his chair and said, "how many times are you going to ask us before you finally believe us!? If we were lying to you we'd be naked by now!"

"Calm down, halfling," the angel replied, "I'll ask as many times as it takes until you tell me the truth. I know that you wear layers of the same clothing, which lets you lie multiple times and get away with it."

The sun was almost set.

"I don't have enough layers to lie to you all day!" exclaimed Vete.

It was true. We had been sitting in the room almost all day with the same angel asking us questions. He had split us up and asked us what happened and when, followed by specifics and cross examinations. Some questions were only asked to Vete and some only to me. This was our first time being questioned together.

"Why do you think it's impossible for a demon to get in here!? Even Satan went to heaven!" Vete almost shouted.

The sun set. The room was dark.

"Can we get a light on?" I asked.

"I have the suggestion letter from the CIC," said Professor.

The what?

"Yes I just got that, too," said the angel.

What? When? How?

"The letter states," began the angel, "that if you can prove to us how a demon entered this facility, we'll believe you. Furthermore, if you can locate and capture this alleged demon and its accomplice and bring them here, then that will avert any war over the item called the Holy Grail, if it even exists."

If?

"Furthermore," continued the angel, "it says that you will begin your first mission soon. The scrolls will be picked up by Professor. You may leave now."

"Yes, sir," I said, "hope you have great night."

When Professor opened the door to the hotel I was almost blinded by the light. We walked down the spiral walkway a few feet before Vete spoke up.

"What was that about!?" he asked in frustration.

Professor scratched his head. "Well," he began, "that angel was a cherub. Cherubs are the wisest of angels and in all their great wisdom they do things, differently. Actually they facilitate all of this, the training room, CBA HQ, all of it. The CIC is ran by cherubs. They employ a network of seraphs for mass communication. That's how the cherub and I received the suggestion letter from the CIC. Seraphs can communicate via telepathy."

"Okay," I said, "that explains how y'all got a 'letter' I never saw y'all get, but why were we questioned and cross examined all day?"

"Cherubs have a hard time trusting humans, wether they've been chosen to be a Class B or not."

"Halflings," I said.

"Yes," he continued, "and even that was a compliment, Tekon. Although I imagine he took a kinder approach to you because you have four wings as well."

"Really?" I asked.

"Yes," he answered, "some angels call you Cherub Junior. Cover your face with your top two wings and you just might pass as one."

"Why do cherubim distrust humans so much?" asked Vete.

"Well," said Professor, "that dates back to Adam and Eve. Cherubs have watched man fall and betray one another since the beginning of time. On top of that, most angels are not merciful, you know. Righteous anger flows quickly through us. Most will dish out punishment the moment something is done wrong."

"Yes, I'm well aware," I said, thinking of Hunter, "some hold grudges."

"Yes some do," said Professor, "which is why I would advise not angering an angel, especially an employee of the CIC like you did."

"I thought only the high up angels were in the CIC," said Vete.

"The only angels allowed in CBA HQ are CIC employed angels," said Professor.

"Oops," I said.

"Why didn't the angel take your word then?" asked Vete.

"Well that dates back before mankind and before time began," said Professor, "the only cherub ever to have fallen was Lucifer, you know. The rest who fell were lesser angels, Levis Tergum as we're called among the angel community, but not all of them rebelled against the Almighty by choice. Some were tricked, but the majority were controlled."

"By music?" I asked.

"Music is a heavenly element," said Vete, "music is not a human invention. It's powers are still beyond human understanding. More precisely, Lucifer had power over sound, correct?"

"Yes, Vete," said Professor, "While Lucifer was to use that power to create music to worship and glorify God, there was also the darker side to his power."

"There's a room on Earth with sound at negative nine decibels," said Vete, "the longest anyone has been able to stay in that room is forty-five minutes."

"Wow," I said, "why not?"

"People go crazy from not being able to hear their own voice, and hallucinate as well," said Vete.

"The power of sound and music go much beyond what humans have figured out," said Professor, "but the CIC, in all its wisdom, refuses to see that. They treat Levis Tergum as second class, just above humans and now above Class B Angels. They treat the seraphs as equals because seraphs have never fallen. They call those who fell demons, but we call them Reikokuna Maero. Since fighting is forbidden between angels, we Levis Tergum call the higher angels seraphs and cherubs instead of seraphim and cherubim. It's petty, but it's all we can do."

"Wait. La cuca-what? Racha?" I asked.

"Reikokuna Maero," said Vete, "Professor, why are we getting our first mission now before we graduate?"

"I don't know," said Professor, "but your skills must be seen as proficient enough to forgo the rest of the training period and advance to missions."

We stopped at the hotel lobby. Through the glass revolving doors I could see people being chased and gunned down.

"I'll go retrieve your mission scrolls," said Professor, "I'll be back by sunrise."

"Yes, sir," I said.

Professor walked out the door into the chaos as if it were a warm sunny day rather than a dark hellish night.

"So this is the adventure," I said, "the suite life of Vete and Tekon."

"What are you talking about?" asked Vete.

"Just a show," I said, "I forgot you didn't grow up with TV."

Vete had been raised in a very conservative Christian home. Though he did have a TV in his home, there was no cable or satellite. He and his family only used it to watch extremely family friendly movies or home videos they made. Each room in Babel Hotel had a TV as well, but Vete refused to watch any shows. I, on the other hand, caught up on shows my human body had probably not been watching anymore.

"Wanna go eat?" I asked, "I probably won't be getting any sleep tonight anyways."

"Sure," he said.

We walked down to the restaurant section. For whatever reason, chosens were given free meals in Babel Hotel and I took advantage of the hospitality. There were countless restaurants. Each had a theme based on a country. Over the month I had tried Egyptian, Indian, French, Brazilian and many more types of food. All of the food was exquisite. I said I was going on a world tour of food, but tonight I wanted to go back to my roots and have a nice American meal. I had an amazing bacon cheeseburger, but Vete simply had a slice of sopapilla cheesecake.

"Not hungry?" I asked.

"Shouldn't eat a big meal this late at night," Vete said.

"True, true, I guess."

"Do you plan on being a vigilante tonight?"

Vigilante. Throughout the month I would leave the hotel at night to save as many people as I could. I could not sleep, anyway. When everyone was gone my mind would drift to my failure to save her, but the city which needed saving was a great distraction. It also gave me a goal to accomplish: to make a difference like the girl before me had. Sleepless nights were what contributed to my low testing scores when I tested solo. The first few nights there were other chosens acting alone. Perhaps they had sadness and depression to escape from as well, or maybe they felt the need to try to save the city, or it could have been both. I managed to round them up and organize us into a team. After a while, the job became too much to do every night and people started losing moral. They felt as if what we did made no difference. At one point, when the group, Anima's Next Heroes, was about to disband, I told them the

story of Vete and I at the church, and what officer Torres had told me about a chosen who
came before us and made a significant difference. They agreed to stay and fight, but we
had to have more people so we could not have
everyone out all night every night. Unfortunately, we all knew no one would fight for a seemingly hopeless cause or else they would already be out. So we took shifts. With the group
being fourteen strong, we were able to have
just two people a night. I also set it up to have
rotating partners. The nights I was not out saving lives I stayed busy exploring the many sections of Babel Hotel to keep from thinking of
Reagan and being depressed. Anima's Next
Heroes was a private group at first, but word
got around about us. We received both praise
and criticism. Some people were even against
what we were doing and there was a division
among the chosens between those who supported Anima's Next Heroes and those who did
not. The only neutral among the chosens was
Vete.

"Not tonight," I said, "not my night. I
went last night."

"How was it?"

"I saw Gabriella again. The girl from the
church? She recognized me before I recognized her."

"You rescue her again?"

"Yeah, but funny thing was that I saw
those goofy guys again. Gus and Shawn? Ac-

tually I've seen them a lot on my nights. I think they're undercover cops, because every time I see them they're either stalling before doing something criminal or they have an outburst at a time when whatever gang they're with would want to stay silent. Then I do my thing and they run away before the cops come."

"Did you see Alejandro?"

"No, not since that one time at the church."

"Did you talk to Gabriella or her grand-mother?"

"I talked to Gabriella, but I haven't seen her grandma since the church event either, but she says she's still alive."

"How often do you see her?"

"Why? You thinking about meeting her? You like her?"

"I believe you do."

"You didn't answer the question, which I'll be sure to ask again and again to be sure you're telling the truth."

"If I lie about something, but then tell the truth about it, the layer returns."

"Good point. I'll just go with you like her and have been thinking about her since we left the church."

"Tekon."

"Yeah?"

"You didn't deny my statement."

"You didn't answer my question."

We could tell when sunrise was approaching because many Citizen Souls started leaving the area. Though I could not see where they were going because they used the traveling tunnels, I knew they headed to the religious section to pray for the families of those who lived outside the hotel. Vete and I flew to the lobby. Professor walked through the revolving doors just as the morning light flashed. If one girl could do all this, I thought, then surely a team could do much, much more.

"If one can put a thousand to flight ...," said Vete.

Was Vete reading my mind? In his hands, Professor held two scrolls. Each scroll had two poles. My scroll was Egyptian blue and Vete's was white. I thanked Professor and we simultaneously opened our scrolls. Mine read:

Dangel Wease
5'11" ~ 03-28/1997
152 lbs. ~ 1433 Terrace Street, Blue Springs, MO, 64015 USA
Your dual mission, should you choose to accept it:
Find the alleged demon who allegedly infiltrated CBA HQ.
Find the angel accomplice of said demon.
Bring both subjects in for questioning.

A dual mission was unheard of, un-precedented, among CBA's. There was no way one person could be a guardian angel and complete those objectives at the same time. Being a guardian angel was a full-time position. I would have asked about the mission objectives, but it was CBA law to keep all mission information private until after the mission was over.

"I must warn you, before you accept the mission," said Professor, "as you know, under normal circumstances you must simply complete your mission, however long it takes. Under these circumstances, the CIC has given you a time limit on your missions. You each have 168 hours to complete your missions."

"Does that include the thirty minutes we have to find the replica of the human we're guarding?" asked Vete.

"No," answered Professor, "once you accept your mission by tapping on the human's name, you will have the regular half hour to find the replica in the city. The map of the city will appear as normal. Once the time limit is up, you will instantly be transported to CBA HQ. If you complete your mission before time is up, simply tap on the human's name again to end the mission and you will be transported to CBA HQ."

"How does the scroll know if we really completed our mission or not?" I asked, "what if we are really close to completing our missions and need more time?"

"It's an honor system, Tekon," said Vete, "we learned about this the day you overslept. As for more time, I think it's safe to say we'd have to make a plea to the CIC or the big man himself. And since the CIC don't believe us about any of this, even Professor who has seen my memories, I doubt we'll be granted more time by the CIC."

"Well, I must be off," said Professor, "don't want to be late again."

"See ya, sir," I said as he walked off, "Well, Vete, I guess I'll see you on the flip side."

I decided to first head to my room and grab my crystals. The moment I saw my bed I instantly felt drowsy. I grabbed my two crystals from a chair and put them in the straps on the inside of my sleeves. I had straps sewn into the inside of my sleeves one night by a member of Anima's Next Heroes as a way of saying thanks for saving her from a falling car. After strapping my crystals I fell onto the bed and thought I would take a short nap before starting my mission. If only I had noticed the white x glowing on my glove before I placed my palm on the soft pillow.

"Wake up, neophyte. Wake up."

I recognized the voice. I opened my eyes, stretched and yawned.

"How long was I asleep?" I asked.

"I've let you slumber in my presence twenty minutes."

"Oh great, just what I needed. A power nap. Sorry to come in here on accident."

"Neophyte, this mission you're going on, you've been set up to fail."

"I know. There's no way I can do all of that in one week, and since it's my first mission I'm also supposed to be learning from whatever angel I'm partnered with, but I'm not worried about that. My main goal, once I get back to Earth, is finding Reagan."

"Your lost friend."

"Yes, sir. I don't have any clear, for-sure, leads, but I have possible clues. Wait, how did you know about my mission?"

"I see everything you see, neophyte."

"That's..."

"Regardless, I need you to go back to where you first heard the demon and angel converse."

"Mr. Vadallat, who are you? When do I get to actually see you? I can't be having too many voices in my head with no faces."

"You shall see me soon enough, once your spiritual potency increases."

"Okay. Yes, sir. What exactly am I supposed to find there? What are you hoping that I find?"

"Begone."

The maroon atmosphere faded away and I was laying on top of my bed. I was about to drift to sleep again when I heard another voice.

'Be safe, Tekon,' the soft, gentle voice echoed inside my head.

For whatever reason, the voice reminded me about Anima's Next Heroes. I would need someone to cover my next shift if I was gone all week. Without cellphones or email or social media it was harder to contact people. Each room had a phone, but people were rarely in their rooms. I picked up the phone on the coffee table and dialed a few numbers, but there was no answer. The sixth dial finally worked.

"Tekon?" came the girl's voice.

She sounded as if she had just woken up. I had called all the guys first because I would not want any girl to be out there at night if it was not necessary, but there were only six guys in the group, including me, and none of them answered. I figured they were probably at training with the rest of the chosens.

"Bonjour, Estelle. Sorry to wake you when you just got back from your shift."

"No, no. ... It is okay."

Estelle was French, had short dark hair which went just past her ears and curled up. She had brown eyes, pink feathered wings coated in diamond, wore a pinkish white robe and wore clear crystal high heels. Her sword was pink with a heart shaped crest on the hilt.

"I need a favor to ask you," I said, "I need you to take my shift this upcoming week."

"Tekon? Are you alright?"

"Yeah, I just may be out of town this week."

"What do you mean, 'out of town?' Where are you going?"

"It's business. Beatrice was supposed to be my partner this time, so be sure to tell her that when you see her. If I get back before my shift would normally be, then I'll do my shift, but if I get back after you've done my shift, then I'll take yours with Katniss."

"Oh Tekon, if you want to spend more time with Katniss, all you must do is say so. Are you two, lovers?"

"Good Lord, Estelle! What the crud!? No! I just need you to fill in for me and if I get back in time then I'll fill in for you rather than having you go back out there twice in a week! Good Lord!"

"Such a strong reaction to such a simple question, Tekon, but I will let Beatrice and Katniss know of your plans. I hope your business goes well. Should I be expecting Katniss to have 'business,' too?"

"What the crud! Estelle!"

She laughed and said, "Oh Tekon you are just too easy to tease, ladies' man. Well, I suppose I should get up now and go to training. I hope your business runs smoothly."

"Thanks. If I don't get back in time for your regular shift, I owe you."

"Yes, you will, and you better be back in time for our ceremony."

The ceremony. Anima's Next Heroes decided to meet in the city and all fight together again on the last night of training. We would fight from sunset to sunrise and make our vows to keep following our schedules I had developed, then once a year we would meet up on the same night and fight together again from sunset to sunrise. Of course, we had to establish how time runs in CBA HQ as compared to Earth and then what GMT time sunset starts, but I said I would figure it out.

"Yes, I'll be there. If not, I'll owe everyone."

She hung up. I walked out the door and flew to the bottom of the hotel. To my surprise, I heard a yawn beside me as I flew down.

"Well hello, Tekon," said Estelle with a wink and a smile. Her robe did not fall down as we flew headfirst due to the angelic nature of our clothing always keeping us modest.

"Bonjour, Estelle."

When we reached the chosens I flew straight to the tunnel. Once I made the first turn, I saw Vete leaning against the wall with his arms folded and I jumped.

"I was wondering when you'd get here," he said.

"How'd you know?'

"I'm pretty sure we have the same missions, Tekon. We were both there when they got the telepathy letter. We may be guarding different people, but I'm pretty sure our missions are at least similar."

"That makes sense. If they are the same, then you know that a large part of this is gonna depend on you."

"I don't know the range at which I can perform Angel Dance, but I'll try my best. More than speed, it's a matter of concentration and patience. Patience is not my strong point."

"Well that's ironic. You have little patience and wanted super speed, but with it you have to have even more patience, 'cause when you go super fast it's like time is almost frozen, right? So you're constantly waiting on everything."

"Precisely."

We walked down the dark tunnel until we reached where we heard the voice and demon.

"It'll be hard to see further on," said Vete, "take out your sword."

We were thinking the same thing.

"Jesus wept."

Psalm 119:10 KJV says 'Thy word is a lamp unto my feet, and a light unto my path.' While on Earth the meaning of everything in the bible may not be so literal, in this world things seemed to work slightly different. My sword created a very dark light since it was a black sword, but the white x was very bright and shined ahead. The only thing ahead of us was a wall. Vete touched the wall we were facing as if to search for a hidden button to push. Immediately electric blue light escaped the edges of the wall and a picture of a galaxy appeared, taking up the entire wall.

"Dude," I said.

Vete touched the picture and the image zoomed in where he had touched. Our solar system was in view. He then touched Earth and then America.

"I'm going to assume the CIC don't know about this," I said.

"Perhaps," said Vete.

He slowly bent his head and leaned into the picture. His head went through it, followed by the rest of his body. The picture went blank, the light faded and I was alone. My heart began to race. I stood still, heart pounding for what seemed like an eternity, before Vete walked out of the wall as if he were a ghost.

"That's how the demon got in," said Vete.

When we walked out of the tunnel, Estelle was standing at the entrance. The other chosens were talking and flying around.

"You know," she said to me as Vete flew away, "if I did not know any better, I would say you and Vete share a special 'business' together, no?" She winked at me as she said 'business.'

I shook my head fiercely. "Oh my-what the holy crud, Estelle!? No! NO! No! I don't roll that way! Good Lord, no! That was just part of my business."

"If you say so, Tekon. Do not make Katniss jealous, yeah?" Another wink.

"Oh my-good Lord, Estelle! I'm not even sure-well, you never know. I mean, there's atheists and Hindus here. I'm pretty sure Daryl is either gay or effeminate, and Serenity, I promise to God she's psycho in a dangerous way."

"Oh Tekon, so harsh with the judging and backstabbing."

"Um, I'm just saying my opinion. You've seen Daryl, which one day I'll talk to him about that, and even you're scared to be alone with Serenity."

She shook her head and said, "yeah, you have a good point there."

"Well anyways, I gotta head out now. I'll see y'all soon."

"If you wish to say bye to Katniss first, she is in the vacation section enjoying a nice spa and sauna." She winked again as she spoke.

"What!?"

She laughed. "I am only kidding. She went to the book store in the shopping section to find me this book she has been going on about. Beatrice went with her as well. Apparently their names are based off of characters in the books."

"What's your name based off of?"

She smiled and said, "maybe one day, Tekon. You have business to attend to first."

"What!? Come on! You can't just mention something and then-well actually I mentioned it. Oh well. Alright. See y'all soon."

I flew off before she could tease me more. Once I was outside the hotel I tapped the name on my scroll. A picture of my human appeared and a holographic view of the city projected from the scroll showing me as a black dot and Dangel as a red dot. We shared the same skin tone. I flew in the sky and followed the map to the west side of the city. A block away from the docks was an arcade called Westside Arcade. It was a grey building and the title was in big yellow letters on top of the entrance. Inside, the arcade was dark and full of techno music, arcade games and a pizza buffet.

"And so," I heard a loud voice say, "the fool comes up to me, and says 'sir?'"

I began walking towards the voice.

"And I said 'what?' and he starts gettin' on his knees."

I found the source of the voice at a table. It was Dangel. He sat in a booth surrounded by other people leaning in to hear every word he said.

"And he says, 'master I-I-I'm sorry. Please don't send me away!' And I mean at this point he's cryin' and sobbin' and I say 'Jenkins! Get a grip and shine my shoes!'"

The crowd laughed, but I failed to see what was so funny.

"Dangel Wease," I said loudly.

The crowd fell silent. He stood, wearing a creme suit with a white tee-shirt and no tie. He walked over to me with a scowl on his face.

"Look," he began, "I ain't seen you around here before so I'm'a cutchu some slack and introduce myself to you properly. 'Cause since you know my name you've at least heard of me, but you obviously ain't heard enough, Otaku. So, people call me D. I don't like Dangel. My mother was drunk when I was born and called me a drunken angel. So call me D. Second, you're in the wrong place at the wrong time. Otaku anime freaks LARP tomorrow and that's in basement four, not the first floor. So go on home and run to mommy and let her wipe your tears, okay? Bye now."

He waved his hand at me.

"Dangel," I said, "you gotta give respect to get it."

I touched my finger to his chest, where his heart would be. The techno music was replaced with screeches. The pizza smell was replaced by the smell of the freshly cut grass I was standing on. There was a beautiful brown mansion in front of me, but before I could take in the grandeur of it all I was struck from behind. I was not hit hard, but hard enough to grab my attention. I turned around to see a giant man with short curly brown hair who wore a red and brown vertically striped robe. He wielded a large spear and was fighting a swarm of Sin, which was called a temptation.

"Don't just stand there lollygagging," said the man in an Irish accent, "help me fight off this temptation!"

A Sin came in my direction only to be swatted down by my blade.

"Interesting summoning verse," said the giant angel after he impaled a row of Sin and stabbed his spear to the ground.

The Sin laid there stacked like a kabob and struggled for life. I guessed he was going to be my partner for guarding Dangel Wease. I hoped the real Dangel was much nicer than the replica in Anima Nex Vita. I looked at the ground to see my defeated Sin unconscious. Another temptation was on its way.

"My name's Chemron," he said as he shrunk closer to my size.

He was still a large man as he held out a muscular arm with an outstretched hand for me to shake. I shook his hand. Normally, when I shook hands with people, I had a firm grip, but Chemron's grip made mine seem like a baby grabbing a grown man's finger.

"Hello, sir. I'm Tekon."

"Nice to meet you, Tekon. This here is Mountain Peak," he said as he gestured towards his still giant spear.

I quickly made up a name for my weapon and said, "this is Lord's Tear."

"Fitting," he said.

He then went on to explain things about Dangel Wease and what types of temptations and Sin he was allowed to face and what types we were to guard him from. All Sin looked the same, but they differentiated by the spiritual pressure they exerted. When Chemron finished off the unconscious Sin, the oncoming temptation's screeches could be heard.

"Since this be your first time," said Chemron, "I'll go ahead and knock this one out for you."

"Uh, thank you sir."

Temptations flew in a triangular formation with the strongest in the lead. I could sense the leading Sin's power was far above mine. The spiritual pressure felt like someone had hit me with weights.

Chemron grew to his normal size and lunged his spear forward yelling, "Mountain Strike!"

His spear made contact with the lead Sin and a single beam of light went through every Sin in the temptation while still connected to the tip of the spear. The beam of light retracted back into the spear and every Sin fell.

"Sin dissolve in an hour once they're dead," said Chemron.

I nodded my head. His eyes stared off into the distance and he was silent for a while. I looked where he was looking, but saw nothing.

"I guess you have new help coming," said Chemron.

"Sir?"

"The CIC has told me to report to the Holy One. So I guess you will have someone coming to replace me to help you."

"Yes, sir," I said, but I knew no one would be coming.

"Well, Lord bless you, Tekon."

He took a few steps away from me and began to fade away until he was no longer visible. So there I was, alone, in a yard full of Sin. Sure enough, an hour went by and the Sin dissolved from existence. As I figured, there was no replacement for Chemron. I was set up to fail, but I had my own goals to achieve. Reagan. Chemron had told me about Dangel's sleeping patterns. He went to bed pretty early. So I flew around and napped in a nearby tree until the evening. When I awoke, the sky was darkening. Dangel had to be asleep, so I took to the skies. If I was going to fail this mission, I was going to use every bit of available time searching for Reagan. The demon had told the voice to be ready when Greed wanted him. When I was in the hospital, I had felt really greedy about the police officer's badge and gun. So the demon had to be close. I did not know where they would be exactly, but I knew the Sin had to be coming from somewhere and I hoped it would be where Greed was.

Chapter 8

The blue crystal lit up whenever there was Sin nearby, so I flew high in the sky since Sin were everywhere. Unfortunately, I got lost in the sky. Thankfully, it did not take long for my crystal to begin glowing again. The crystal glowed so bright it was almost blinding so I slid it back in my sleeve. I could not see anything different about the area I was in and I felt the spiritual pressure from so many Sin down below I was almost numb to the common pressure, but suddenly I saw it. There was a bright blue outline of a rectangle, just like the one Vete and I had discovered earlier, floating in the sky. Within the rectangle were countless Sin inside what looked to be a cave. I could see their mouths open and close, but I could not hear any screeches.

I flew up to the picture in the sky. Every Sin's eye was trained on me. I summoned Lord's Tear and prodded at the picture. My sword poked through and Sin backed away from it, but I still could not hear their screeches. I pulled my sword out of the portal and flew around it, but on the other side the portal was nonexistent. It could only be seen from one side and could only be entered from one side. When I came back around a claw swiped at me, but I blocked it. An enormous spiritual pressure hit me as if bags of sand were dumped on top of me. I faced a powerful Sin. The claw grabbed my sword and pulled me into the swarm. The moment my ears passed the barrier of the portal I could hear the deafening screeches. The smell of tar and sulfur filled my nostrils. I could feel countless claws groping me everywhere. Struggling was useless. I felt stretched as if I was being pulled in every direction. The Sin carried me somewhere, led by the big one who was the only one to touch Lord's Tear. I tried to move Lord's Tear back and forth to cut the big Sin's hand, but it had such a powerful grip I could not move it an inch. Why was this one not hurt by Lord's Tear?

Soon the screeches became rhythmic for a short while and I was dropped on the ground, but the big Sin and I refused to let go of Lord's Tear so my arm was raised. The screeches stopped.

"On your knees, cherub," said a man's voice.

I looked up to see a pig laying on a golden throne glaring at me. I had to catch myself before I burst out in laughter, but further gazing showed the pig to look rather delicious. It would make good bacon. A ham sandwich would not be so bad either. The throne looked pretty sweet, too.

"On your knees, I said," came the voice again.

It seemed to be coming from the pig. The big Sin yanked me up to my knees.

"I'm pretty sure this situation is supposed be switched around," I said with a chuckle, "and you're supposed to be on a plate in very thin slices with some barbecue sauce."

The pig leaped from his throne and walked towards me. As it did, it morphed into a dark grey wolf. The wolf stopped inches from my face and growled.

"You must want to suffer a very painful eternity," came the voice again.

It was definitely this creature speaking to me and not some man behind a machine. I wanted his fur. His fangs would make a nice necklace, too. Wait. Since when did I wear necklaces? The wolf paced back and forth for a while before finally asking me how I found him. I wanted a wolf. No. I needed to focus. What was this feeling of wanting to have everything I saw? I had felt it before, but ... the throne. It looked pretty awesome.

"Can I have your throne?" The words blurted out before I could even think about the answer to his question.

The wolf stopped and glared at me.

"Oh," he said with disappointment in his voice, "you must be Tekon."

The sound of my Class B name snapped me out of the sensation.

"How do you know my name?" I asked.

The sensation tried to creep over me again like a warm blanket on a cold night, but I fought it off. I had felt this before, but where?

"He's expendable," said the wolf to the big Sin, "kill him."

What? Expendable? Like trash? Another big Sin came from somewhere in the cave and stood in front of me as countless Sin held me back. The big Sin drew its arm back with its claws ready. I struggled with all my might, but to no avail. The screeches began again. Lord, I thought, if ever there was a time I needed you right now, right now would be it.

I heard the wolf mutter, "if only ... Vete."

I only caught those words, but the message was clear. Why did he want Vete? Why was Vete worth keeping and not I? The Sin swung its claws.

"Waaaiiiit!"

The Sin stopped, claws inches from my face. The screeches stopped as well.

"Don't kill him now! He has a use!"

The voice. It was the same voice I heard in the forest, the city, the tunnel and the cloudless room in CBA HQ. The traitor angel who had repeatedly tried to kill me had just saved my life.

"What use does this one have?" asked the wolf.

I moved my head to try and see who the wolf was talking to, but all I could see was the wolf facing his throne.

"The Chronos Scindo," said the voice.

"I thought the Chronos Scindo was for Vete," said the wolf.

186

"I have bigger and better plans for that brat," said the voice, followed by hysterical laughter.

The wolf growled and said, "take him to the Chronos Scindo."

The Sin carried me away and the screeches began again. The second big Sin blocked my view of whomever was sitting on the wolf's throne. I let go of Lord's Tear and it vanished. There was no point in resisting. In order to not go crazy from the screeches, I relaxed and concentrated on what all just happened. Soon the screeches were barely a whisper to me.

To recap, the big monkeys could grab Lord's Tear and seemed to be unaffected by it. The telepathic animal was a shapeshifter as well and had a greedy aura surrounding it. The Chronos Scindo was also talked about in the tunnel. What was a Chronos Scindo? In which case, was the shapeshifting animal Greed? I thought only seraphim had the gift of telepathy? Wait. So the soft, gentle voice in my head was a seraph? Was I really not schizophrenic, then? Was Vadallat a seraph? Wait, did the wolf guy know where Reagan was?

'Tekon? Where are you?' The usually gentle voice seemed worried, though still soft.

Again, I was dropped on the ground. I did not realize the screeches had stopped, but I did hear the sound of a gate close and lock behind me. The room of the cave I was in was damp and had a moldy smell along with the tar and sulfur combo. The only object in the room was a large oval-shaped mirror with a sky-blue frame. I walked over to the mirror, when every gamer instinct inside of me told me not to, and at first only saw my reflection from the chest up because of where the mirror was hung on the cave wall. I gazed into the mirror and saw a girl with long brunette hair chained to the cave wall. Her hair covered her face and she was clothed in rags. There were bruises along her arms and what I could see of her legs. My gaze focused on her because I could have sworn her figure was Reagan's. Her head was hung low, but as she looked up at me her hair parted just a little.

"Reagan!" I shouted.

I was going to turn around and run to her, but my reflection lunged out at me through the mirror, shattering the glass, with its hands at my neck. I managed to get both feet under him while he was strangling me and pushed him off of me. The figure which stood before me was my opposite. He looked exactly like me, but the colors were switched. Where I had black, he had white and vice versa. I quickly glanced at where Reagan should have been, but there was no one there.

"Who are you?" I asked.

"I'm you," he replied with my voice.

"No," I said, thinking of a favorite video-game series of mine, "you're my nobody."

"So then do you have my heart?"

We shared the same memories.

"Do you have my weapon?"

He held out his left hand and with a flash of light another color-switched version of Lord's Tear appeared, though the hilt was the same. I summoned Lord's Tear and said its name.

My replica responded with, "God's Wrath."

"Your name," I began, "is your own. Don't take mine."

"You already know what my name will be," he replied.

He was right. I knew exactly what his name would be, because it would be what I would choose were I in the same situation. I would take an x and scramble it into my name.

"X-kneot," we said simultaneously, "X for short."

"X-kneot," said the wolf from outside the gate, "you may now slay Tekon."

X-kneot pointed God's Wrath at me and I pointed Lord's Tear at him. How was I supposed to fight myself?

"Who are you?" asked X-kneot.

"Your new master," said the wolf, "now kill him."

"I need a name," said X-kneot.

"Greed," said the wolf.

Greed! I knew it! The demon named Greed. I stared into X-kneot's hood. There was a vast difference. Inside my hood, people could only see darkness, but inside his hood I only saw white as if his hood were empty, but I did not need to see his face to know what he was thinking.

"Where's Reagan?" we both asked and slashed the black iron gate in an x formation.

The two big Sin stood on either side of the pig who was now standing on his hind legs.

"Kill Tekon," said the pig, "and I will take you to her."

"Crud," I said.

X-kneot brought God's Wrath down upon me, but I blocked and swung my left knee up. He swung his right knee up and our knees collided. I went for a palm to his sternum with my left hand, but I instead collide my palm with his right palm. We both jumped back, stabbed our keys into the ground, twisted and pulled them out. Nothing happened. God's Wrath must have had the opposite effect of Lord's Tear. Where Lord's Tear allowed the user to escape, God's Wrath must prevent the target from escaping. Our abilities canceled each other's out. So it was a matter of who could use the power without the other person knowing. X-kneot quickly stabbed his key into the ground again. I tried to close the distance between us, but he twisted and pulled out before I could reach him. There was a tremor in the ground and stalagmites grew into what seemed like a birdcage around me. I stabbed my key into the ground, twisted and pulled it out. The stalagmite cage shattered and I did not hesitate to use my sword's power again, but neither did X-kneot. I felt a gust of wind for a second, but then it died down. We both realized the futility of using our powers against each other, so X-kneot wasted no time closing the distance and swinging his sword. It was what I would do, but, because I knew what I would do, blocking him was easy.

So we became unpredictable. We threw our weapons at each other, knowing they would collide. We both knew we were denying our first instincts, which made us hesitant in our fight. Instead of a kick, he sent a fist towards my face, but I deflected his punch, grabbed his arm and went for an uppercut. He grabbed my arm so I leaned back, pulling him down with me, and brought up my knees as hard as I could. One landed in his groin. A sharp yelp escaped him and he let go of my arm while trying to wrench his other arm out of my grip, but I quickly grabbed his arm and did not let go of the other. He flapped his wings and became vertical, almost perpendicular to me. I folded my two large wings above me to box his ears, but my wings were blocked by his. Suddenly, he pushed towards me. Since I was already trying to pull in my direction to keep him from escaping, I only accelerated the speed at which his two fists made painful contact with my two cheeks. I felt like my teeth could fall out at any moment. He got on top of me as I fell to the ground and strangled me. I tried wrenching his arms off of me, but they would not budge. Would I really kill someone to find Reagan? As my vision began to fade I sent a fist towards his face. I thought I hit his nose, but he did not let up.

I managed to mumble "Jesus wept" and swung my sword. Whatever I hit got him off of me. I quickly stumbled to my feet, coughing and gasping for air. I stabbed Lord's Tear in the ground and leaned on it. I saw a flash of white and my face stung. I fell to the ground, but my hand stayed on Lord's Tear. I turned it to get a better grip and I watched a white shoe dig into my rib cage.

"Enough!" I yelled.

With newfound strength I stood up and slashed at X-kneot. He blocked the slash, but somehow I had enough force behind me to send him hurtling through the air to the cave wall next to Greed and his two Sin. Greed did not look happy. Next, all I saw was fire, but I felt no heat. As quickly as the fire rose, it died down and I was in the sky again. The fresh air was a relief to my nostrils.

'Tekon! Where are you!? You need to get back to your human!'

The soft voice sounded panicked. What had happened while I was gone? I thought Dangel was asleep. Who can sin in their sleep? Before me was the gateway to the cave

I was just in. The cave seemed empty at first, but soon a small Sin came into view and opened its mouth. Soon more Sin came into view, followed by X-kneot. He slowly walked through the crowd of Sin. Behind him was Greed and his two big Sin. I wished I could close the gate somehow. I slowly walked backward in the sky. X-kneot walked out of the portal.

"We both want to find Reagan," I said.

"But you're standing in the way," said X-kneot as he summoned God's Wrath.

"You know you can't beat me," I said, "because my power comes from within. And greater is He that is in me, than he that is in the world. If God be for me, who can be against me?"

"Yes I know where your power comes from, but you have to understand this as well. I am you. As you grow stronger, so will I. I'm not a simple clone that's not connected to you in any way. I'm a part of you that's forever linked with you."

"How?"

"It doesn't matter!"

X-kneot flew at me ready to strike. I flew up, flipped forward and came down with a right heel kick. He blocked with his right arm and swung his sword in his left hand to cut my leg off. I swooped my right arm down and swung up, catching his sword in my x. I put my right foot on his shoulder and jumped, but he grabbed my leg and swung me down. So down I flew. He followed.

"If you're linked to me then you know what happens to you if I die!" I shouted.

When he got within range I swung at him. He blocked and I decided to keep him on the defensive. I kept swinging at him until I noticed the grassy field below us. I hooked his sword with my x and flung him to the ground. He recovered and landed on his feet. I came at him from above with a slash, but he blocked with God's Wrath. I flipped backwards in the air and slowly descended in front of him.

"I won't die if you die," he said, "I'll continue to live on."

"So you have your own soul?"

"That's not important."

"Yes it is. You know you need a soul."

"That's not what I meant."

"What do you mea-oh, you're just not gonna tell me any more information about it. So Greed explained to you how that all works, huh?"

"That and other things. There is one edge I have over you, though."

He swung his sword at me, which I thought was silly because I was nowhere near his range, but suddenly a powerful wind hit me and blew me off my feet. I steadied myself in the air and heard a loud roar coming from his direction, but not from him.

"You get wishes, too?" I asked.

It was the only possible explanation. For chosens, the second wish was for an animal God created, but did not put on Earth.

"Why ask questions in which you already know the answer to?" asked X-kneot.

Of course X-kneot had wishes, and he used his second one.

In training we were told our first wish could be used at any time after we graduated training and the first wish did not have to be used before the remaining two. The second wish could be used only after the completion of ten missions and after we had slain one hundred Sin. So far, I had slain none and I had not even finished my first mission, but if he summoned what I thought he summoned, I was not going to make it out of there alive if I did not summon something as well.

My guess was he summoned a wind dragon. Wind dragons were twenty feet tall when standing on their hind legs. Their wingspans were thirty feet and the tails were ten feet long, making the beasts thirty feet long when stretched out flying. They had the ability to bend light around them to become invisible when summoned. They always stayed within a mile radius of their master. They freely controlled wind and granted their master control over wind as well. Needless to say, wind dragons were my first choice. I could have tried to escape, but God's Wrath was inescapable almost. So I had to ask.

"Will you let-?"

"Of course," interrupted X-kneot, "go ahead and use your second wish."

Summoning another wind dragon would have been pointless, so I racked my brain for the next best thing, which I assumed X-kneot did as well. Lord's Tear in hand, I wished for my creature. X-kneot laughed so hard I wondered if I made the right choice.

Cuddling up to my legs was a black, four-legged, nine-tailed creature with small white feathered wings on its back, electric-blue tipped tails with an electric-blue ring near the end of each tail and electric-blue eyes. It could not have been much more than a foot tall, perhaps fourteen inches. It had a cute round face like a cat, but there were no whiskers and it had the body of a fox. The wings being white meant it was a girl, otherwise it would have had black wings.

The creature was actually classified as the only furry dragon, the dragon part because of its tremendous power. The rings on each of the tails stored electricity which could be released from the mouth and tips of the tails. The tails could also extend and expand on will. Unfortunately, the creatures scared easily and became either paralyzed in fear or ran off. They were easily distracted by shiny things and were very picky about whom they served and when.

When we first learned about creatures God made, but did not put on Earth, the furry dragons were said to be the worst choice a chosen could choose as a partner. They were considered to be worse than a grasscarp, which was a fish (much like a carp) which could only survive on land by transforming into a blade of grass. The rare ones could transform into a flower or possibly a tree, but the tree transformation was even more rare.

The creature was sitting by me with two of her tails wrapped around my legs. I chose her because I believed I could grow a bond with her and make her face and overcome her fears. Then she would be completely loyal to me.

"Electra, electrify," I said.

She only looked at me and began to scratch her head with her hind leg.

"Well," chuckled X-kneot, "it looks like Electra is loafing around!"

Another video-game reference.

"Zenith," said X-kneot, "I think a simple air slash will suffice."

I grabbed Electra and jumped to the air, narrowly dodging a powerful blast of wind which split the ground where I was standing. I held Electra to my chest and all nine of her tails wrapped around me tightly. X-kneot, with an incredible boost in speed, flew to me with God's Wrath ready to impale Electra and I. I could feel Electra's heart begin to race and mine did as well. There was no time to dodge. Electra let out a cry, which sounded like a flute, and a beam of electricity shot out of her mouth. The blue light struck X-kneot right on the black x with such force he was thrown back down to the ground. His dragon roared and a powerful gust of wind slammed Electra and I to the ground. I landed on my back. The pressing wind did not let up and it became hard to breathe. I tried to fold my wings over us, but the wind was too powerful for me to lift them. Darkness began to cloud my vision until I could only see black. I could no longer feel the wind though I could still hear it.

An electric blue light appeared above me and illuminated the space I was in. It looked like a dark dome with ridges. The dragon roared outside the dome. Electra was breathing frantically. I petted her on her head and sat up. I realized I was inside a dome created by Electra's tails.

"Thanks, girl," I said.

Perhaps they were all wrong about furry dragons. I began to wonder if Zenith's wind was hurting Electra, but if it did she showed no sign of it. Would God's Wrath hurt her? Thinking of my next move, I sat and watched Electra as she played with the tip of her tail which was illuminating the dome. She was not scared into paralysis so far, and she had yet to run off, so she could handle a bit of stress. Did she understand human speech? English? I became distracted and began to examine Lord's Tear. I noticed Electra looking at it with curious eyes.

She poked her tongue out and slowly moved her mouth toward Lord's Tear.

"Don't touch," I said softly.

She stopped and looked at me as if to ask if I was serious about my command.

"Do you understand me?" I asked.

She licked my hand and I could feel her tongue through my fingertips. I wondered if my gloves worked the reverse way as well. Could she feel my fingertips through the gloves? The wind stopped and Electra's ears perked up. I stood and slowly watched the stars in the night sky begin to fill the air again as Electra retracted her tails. I stabbed Lord's Tear in the ground for good measure, then looked around to find Electra and I surrounded by countless quiet Sin. There was a deep circular ditch surrounding us as well, courtesy of Zenith. In front of me, at the edge of the other side of the ditch was Greed in pig form standing on his hind legs, his two big Sin on either side of him, and X-kneot hunched over with his hand to his chest behind him. God's Wrath was nowhere in sight. Electra quickly jumped onto my chest and wrapped her tails around me.

"You chosens are always a hassle," said Greed, "should've killed you when I had the chance, but it looks like I have that chance again." Greed jumped over the ditch, landed as a wolf and began to circle me. "Do you know how I came to be in this cursed form?" he asked. I shook my head and kept a steady hand on Lord's Tear. "Hmph. So they don't teach about me up there. Then let me explain this to you before you die. Your final gift in this life. Many years ago, a chosen aided by a seraph found my lair. Are you being aided by a seraph, Tekon? Any voices in your head, now and then, telling you things?"

So I was not the only one. There was another, too. I did not know how to respond to his question. If I lied, I would be revealed, but if I told the truth, then what?

"Your hesitation about how to answer confirms it," said Greed.

"It's a girl," said X-kneot, "haven't met her yet, though."

"A girl?" asked Greed. He chuckled and said, "well, so she's at it again. After I kill you, Tekon, I'll be sure to kill her as well this time. Moving on, I was in a much more powerful form when this young chosen challenged me, but the girl, alas, defeated me." A girl? Was she the same girl I had been hearing about? The girl from Anima Nex Vita? "After which she used a peculiar power to transform me into a pig, and then a wolf for her pet. She laughed as she destroyed my Sin factory and killed all but two of my Necrosin. Her cockiness is what later became her downfall, but I still cannot regain my original form. In this cursed form I am physically harmless, but she did not know of my other power."

"What are Necrosin?" I asked.

He stopped and said, "the two behind you."

Behind me? Something struck me in the back of both knees and I went down on my knees, eye level with Greed. My two large wings and arms were grabbed. Yellow symbols appeared on the ground. He slowly walked over to me and placed his paw on Electra's head. Electra began to cry as if in pain as the yellow symbols on the ground migrated to Greed and then to Electra.

"You see," said Greed, "the chosen girl who put me in this form was unaware of my knowledge of Reikokuna Alchemy." The electric-blue color on Electra turned yellow. "And with Reikokuna Alchemy, I'm more dangerous than you'd think."

Chapter 9

Immediately I felt Greed's aura emanate from Electra. She looked up at me and opened her mouth. I did not wait to see what would come out. I yanked Lord's Tear out of the ground with a twist and hoped the traditional ninety degree turn was not required. Yellow flames quickly erupted and died down just as fast. In front of me stood Dangel's mansion. On the porch stood Professor and Chemron. What was Professor doing there? He and Chemron, who was human size, both looked sad.

'Tekon. Where have you been?' The soft voice sounded sad.

What happened while I was gone? I was only gone one night. I looked down to examine Electra. The yellow light which had possessed her moments before was gone. I petted her as I walked to the two angels. They saw me and began to walk towards me as well. I pulled Electra off my chest and set her down. She began to prance around.

"Where were you?" asked Professor.

A good question. Just where was I a moment ago?

"Answer quickly now, boy," said Chemron.

"I think ..." What was I going to say? Should I say anything? Regardless of where I was or what just happened, I could not forget about the traitor angel and the Holy Grail. I was pretty sure I could trust Professor, but what about Chemron? I must have hesitated too long, because Professor's ominous hand was looming towards me.

"I fought Greed!" the words burst out of my mouth to protect my privacy, "I mean I found his lair." The solidity of my clothing seemed to anger Chemron and sadden Professor.

"Don't lie now, boy," said Chemron as he crossed his arms, "he's a layered one, is he not Professor?"

"No," said Professor as he scratched his head.

"So found his lair, did you?" asked Chemron, "and just how did you do that from here? How'd you find his lair when you were supposed to be guardin' Dangel? Hm?"

"I'll be expecting to hear about this in your trial," said Professor.

Trials. Before Vete and I began our special training in the city we were brought to the courthouse and questioned. It was an interesting process. The jury was a group of lesser angels, Levis Tergum. There were two magistrate cherubim and one arbiter seraph. I had no idea what anyone looked like because we were not allowed to open our eyes, which also meant I had no idea what the inside of the courthouse looked like. We were put on trial for constantly leaving the group and jumping ahead in the lesson and the premature uses of our first wish. I had an extra mark against me for implying the possibility of Hunter telling a lie. Now, with Electra being evidence of my premature use of my second wish and getting caught leaving my post, I was going to be put in a second trial once I returned to CBA HQ.

"Yes, sir," I said, "is Greed still considered a threat, or a minor threat, at least?"

"No," answered Professor, "that's why we don't teach on him. He's been harmless for centuries."

Centuries?

I began, "Well he's-"

Professor held up his hand and said, "we'll hear about it in the trial. Right now I have some bad news for you." What now? "Dangel is dead."

Dead? How? I was only gone for one night!

I began again, "How can-?"

"While you were out flying about and doing who knows what for the past seven days," said an angered Chemron, "Dangel, a newcomer to the Kingdom of the most high God, was left to fight every temptation on His own!" Tears began to fill the angel's eyes. "When I arrived here, this house ... was flooded with Sin." Professor looked at him. "Many apologies," said Chemron to Professor, "it is not fit for human eyes to see angels cry."

Chemron turned and walked back towards the mansion. Electra flew to him and perched on his broad shoulders.

"Tekon," said Professor, "why were you gone for so long?"

"I wasn't, sir. Or at least I though it was just one night."

How was I gone one week? Does time move differently in Greed's lair? Wait. What about my replacement? When Chemron left, he said there must be a replacement. Where was his replacement? I would not have been able to defend Dangel anyway without someone else there who could slay Sin. Where was my replacement?

"Wait, where was my replacement?"

"What replacement?"

"When Mr. Chemron left, he said I must be getting a replacement mentor. Where was my replacement mentor? How was I supposed to protect Dangel from Sin if I could only knock them out?"

"What are you talking about, Tekon?"

Professor's face looked both curious and confused. Something was not right.

"When I first got here, Mr. Chemron was called away by the CIC. Where was his replacement?"

Of course, I remembered, there was never a replacement. I was set up to fail in every way possible no matter what I did. Professor stared at me for a while, but my clothing remained visible.

"I'll look into it," was all he said.

Chapter 10

"The trial of Asanté Tekon Bulivard's abdicating his responsibilities on a mission and precocious use of his second wish will now commence," said a female voice.

I was in the trial, eyes closed as mandated. It was the same female voice as before in my previous trial, but even then it sounded familiar. I heard the flapping of wings and shuffle of feet as everyone, but me, took a seat.

"You may give me your oral report," said she.

"Yes, ma'am," I said.

I told them everything which happened after I had touched the picture on the scroll and accepted my mission. The portal and conversation with Vadallat did not need to be mentioned. At least, not then. I hoped I would not be asked about finding out how someone could have snuck into CBA HQ.

"Young man," said a man's voice. It seemed to be coming from my right. "Is any part of this report truncated?" The third word in the trial I did not understand.

Trying to sound educated, I said, "no part of my actions during my mission was omitted."

"Is your armor layered?" came a man's deep voice from my left. His voice was also familiar beyond my previous trial.

"No, sir," I answered, "my armor is not layered."

They had asked me those same exact questions last time as well. It must be mandatory for every trial.

"Now, we have here," said the first man, "the report from your recent interrogation."

Great.

"As well as the report from your previous trial," said the deep voice.

"Given the amalgamation of these reports and your oral report," said the female voice, "we think it best to proceed with an abdication."

Abdication?

"Because you are a frequent target," said the second voice, "it is best to simply remove you from the equation before the enemy accomplishes whatever goals they have involving you. They have already created the neophyte X-kneot with the Chronos Scindo and their goals for you are unknown, but not likely to be in our favor. Therefore an abdication would be the best for you and the Kingdom."

"However," said the third voice, "that would be fatuous should the enemy choose another target."

"Which," said the female, "is why we are going against our better judgment. It is an act unprecedented."

There was a hint of remorse in her voice when she said the last word.

"As for this Reagan," said the second voice, "she is who you risked your life for on Earth, therefore your pursuit of her is understood, but you must be a staunch guardian angel when on missions. All personal interests come second to the mission objectives."

"Although," said the deep voice, "and I hope to have a galvanizing impingement by saying this, Tekon, someone has demarcated you and Vete above other neo-moieties. Because we are not further delimiting your spiritual nor sacred potency, it has been decided."

"We will concede mission requests regarding your lost friend and this mystery voice," said the female, "also, because this apostate's intentions for you and Vete are unknown, you shall both be under surveillance until the matter is resolved."

Then the three angels said simultaneously, "the trial of Asanté Tekon Bullivard's abdicating his responsibilities on a mission and precocious use of his second wish will now complete."

It was finished. My second trial. The person on trial got one chance to say everything needed to be said, then judgment was passed, yet I had no idea what just happened.

Chapter 11

I opened my eyes after the angels said "complete." I was in my room in Babel Hotel. Electra was curled up on the bed with one eye open looking at me.

"Hey girl," I said.

She went back to sleep.

'We will meet soon, Tekon,' the soft, gentle voice sounded excited as it echoed inside my head.

Just who was this seraph lady? Why was she helping me? Did she know Greed was out to get her? At least I was not suffering from schizophrenia. There was a knock on the door. I peeked through the hole and asked who it was, as if Vete was not the only one who ever knocked on my door. Sure enough, it was Vete. When I opened the door, his eyes immediately fell on Electra.

"The voice?" he asked.

"Yeah," I said as I let him in and closed the door.

"Explain."

So I told him what all had happened since we had parted ways.

There was a moment of silence after telling my story before he finally said, "I think there's two voices."

"What? How?"

He smiled. Words did not reveal the answer to me. From behind Vete, a simian guise walked into view. It looked almost exactly like a Necrosin and was as tall as one, being six feet tall on two legs, but it was white rather than black and had three black stripes near the tip of its tail. Simian guises were pretty much winged monkeys born the size of a pygmy marmoset, but grew up to six feet tall with a five foot long tail. The wingspan of a six foot simian guise was also six feet and the wings were leathery. The fur at birth was grey, but whitened with age. They were also very intelligent. It was because of their superior intelligence, strength, agility and their ability to disappear at will they were not put on Earth.

"Good Lord, Vete! I didn't think you were serious about choosing a simian guise!"

Of course, I had yet to hear Vete tell a joke.

"Have you ever heard me joking?" Well there you go. "I named him Sagacious because he is."

Electra awoke, stretched and stared at Sagacious.

"But from the sounds of it," I began, "I was in Greed's lair for a week, so the voice could've gone to you and had you use a wish as well."

"Maybe, but why the different tactics? The first time we encountered him, there was a trap set up for me. You heard the voice in the city and he used fire. Again, in the desert he used fire. Then, you just encountered him again, but no fire. Instead it was that mirror trap originally meant for me. And when I encountered the voice on my mission, he used fire again. But I'm even more untrusting of the CIC now. You were set up to fail and they didn't mention anything about Chemron being called away. And only the CIC can call angels away like that. You should not have been left alone."

"So the CIC doesn't like me and is willing to sacrifice souls to hell to make me fail."

I was not sure if I was asking Vete for confirmation or telling myself for reassurance. Vete said nothing and we let it sink in.

"There is good news," he finally said.

What possible good news could there be? Someone in the CIC was out to get me and was willing to condemn souls to do it!

"Greed asked you how you found his lair," he said. I sat on the bed and petted Electra's tails. Two of them wrapped around my waist. "That means," he continued, "that he and the voice possibly don't know how the crystals work. Also, the voice is probably a cherub, because you said Greed was looking at his throne when he was talking to him. The only throne I know of in heaven is God's, and only He sits on the throne. The cherubs are constantly around it, but never able to sit on it, so one would think the angel would take the first available chance to sit on a throne."

"But wouldn't every angel want to?"

Vete crossed his arms and closed his eyes, then opened them and said, "you have a good point. That doesn't erase the CIC setting you up."

"Unless the voice infiltrated CIC. And there's still that demon the voice was talking to."

"So then maybe we're not closer to finding out who the traitor is, but you still know where Greed's lair is, and he knows where Reagan is."

"Speaking of which, how do those gates work?"

"I don't know, but I think I know where I can find out."

"Where?"

There was a knock on the door. Electra jumped and hid under the bed. Sagacious disappeared. The only person to ever knock on my door was Vete, so I had no idea who could have been at the door. A look through the peephole showed Professor.

"Who is it?" I asked anyway.

"Professor," he answered.

I slowly opened the door and let him in.

"Ah," he said once he saw Vete, "I presumed you'd be here as well." He scratched his head, looked at me and said, "it's time for your report."

After each mission, assuming the CBA was not put on trial, he or she was supposed to report to the CIC embassy for a visual and written report. If the CBA was put on trial, a written report would have been made during the oral report. Afterwards there was a mandatory Prayer Life, during which the CBA was advised to sharpen the sword, strengthen the armor and help build the Kingdom.

Vete came with us to the CIC embassy in the city. I honestly did not know how I could have missed it after spending so much time in the city. It was a large, shiny golden pyramid in the north end of the city with grey rectangular concrete pillars spiked at the top. The pillars were as tall as the pyramid and supported the light blue glass halo. There was no stairway on the pyramid and the surface was extremely slippery. Electra's eyes lit up as we approached it and she flew straight to it, but found no footing when she tried to stand on one of the walls and quickly slid down before she thought to fly off of it. I flew to the only visible entrance which was a square hole near the top of the pyramid. I flew in and inside were crystals of various colors sticking out from the floor, walls and ceiling as if I was inside a geode.

"Don't touch the crystals," said Professor from outside.

"Hello?" I asked.

"Voice recognized," said a male automated voice, "please state your purpose."

"Visual report," I answered.

"Please name your creature," said a female automated voice.

Why did it want to know what my creature was?

"Furry dragon," I answered as I petted Electra, "female."

"Truth confirmed," said the female automated voice.

Well there you go. The crystals began to shine and many pictures began to display on them. It took a while for me to figure it out at first, but I recognized the images to be my mission as seen through my eyes. I saw Dangel at the arcade on one crystal and Greed circling me as a wolf on another crystal. Each crystal showed different scenes.

"You are being summoned for questioning," said the male automated voice.

Electra began to glow in a white light and separated from me. The electric-blue coloring on her turned white, but she did not appear to be in pain.

"Electra!" I screamed.

I reached out to her, but the moment I touched her she bursted into small white spheres of light which floated around and slowly faded away. I turned around to look at Professor and Vete, but before I could ask them what was going on a transparent pink wall shot up in front of me. I touched it. It was crystal. I turned around to find myself encased in a pink crystal. The world around me twisted and blurred. My stomach wanted to jump out of my mouth and run a marathon. When my distorted vision returned to normal, I only saw clouds. My stomach lowered from my mouth to my throat. The room smelt of mint leafs. A cloud in front of me moved to reveal a female cherub. She wore a light green robe, had long blonde hair and four dark green feathered wings, two of which covered her face. She was sitting at a bamboo desk. Her chair, I assumed, was a giant mint leaf. There was nothing on her desk except a glass of water and her folded hands.

"Asanté," she said. Her voice was soft spoken and soothing, as well as extremely familiar.

"Yes, ma'am?" I answered.

I thought I heard a smile when she said, "my, my."

"Ma'am?"

"Oh nothing." I definitely heard a smile. "Your creature is safe," she continued, "creatures must also undergo visual reports, but that process is quite different."

I nodded my head and said, "Yes, ma'am."

"Do you know where you are right now?"

"No, ma'am."

I tried to imagine what her face looked like.

"You are currently at an entrance to the CIC headquarters. This particular entrance is at the peak of Mount Zenith in the training room."

Mount Zenith?

"Ma'am?"

"Did Hunter not give you a map of the facility?"

"No, ma'am."

She chuckled softly. Her voice sounded so familiar it was on the tip of my tongue where I had heard her voice before. She pulled out a drawer from her desk and from it took out a bamboo scroll and placed it on her desk. It rolled out on its own. I walked over to her desk to look at it. It showed the entire training room as one giant circle with a small circle, Anima Nex Vita, at its center. The outer circle was divided into four sections: the southern forest, the northern mountains, the eastern desert and the western sea. Each section on the map had its own color and central landmark. For the green forest, there was a giant tree in the center. For the tan desert there were ruins surrounding an oasis. For the blue sea I saw a hurricane shown from above. For the dark grey mountains there was a giant mountain with clouds below its peak. For the light grey Anima Nex Vita there was a skyscraper with a giant TV screen on it. Babel Hotel.

"My name is Natura Uxor," she said, "but you may call me Uxor."

"Yes, ma'am."

"And this versi arboris is Ingenium."

"Ma'am?"

She giggled, twirled her hair in her fingers and said, "the shapeshifting plant." I had forgotten. A versi arboris was a shapeshifting plant with no true form. "If you touch a section," said Uxor, "the map will zoom in and I'll explain the attributes to you."

I touched the tree. The tiles on the map flipped over in a ripple effect as if my finger was a stone dropped in a pond. The forest took over the map.

"The entire forest," Uxor began, "is one tree. It is popularly called the tree of life because every plant you see in the forest has its roots connected to it and every plant on Earth can be found in the forest. That does, however, include the carnivorous and poisonous plants as well, but don't worry. All dangerous plants are in the southwestern corner of the forest and are lined by a thicket of hedge apple spikes and upas trees, so you can't miss it. If you go to the top of any central landmark you can see the entire respective zone. Because of the way the training room is divided, from the top of the tree you can also see some of the city and a little of the desert and sea, however the forest has the only landmark where you can see other sections from the top of the central landmark."

"Yes, ma'am."

I forgot the reason why I was there as I began to explore the training room through her map and listened to her explanations. The sea provided water to the neighboring zones. So Anima Nex Vita's water supply, the northern waterfalls and the rivers, streams and lakes of the southern forest got their water from the western sea. The sea also housed every sea creature on Earth. The storm in the center of the sea was full of twisters, lightning and tidal waves. At the eye of the storm was a maelstrom. Neither calamity was the central landmark. The central landmark was the castle at the center of the maelstrom, Vortex. The east and west wings of the castle branched out into Vortex City, an underwater city.

The mountain zone was outlined by mountains with caves and valleys throughout. Mount Zenith was surrounded by a ring of active volcanoes and was constantly struck by red lightning from the ash clouds.

The desert was full of nothing, but sand. Sand dunes and cracked earth was all there was to see, minus the occasional cactus or tumbleweed. The desert housed one of every type of cactus and tumbleweed, but they were all spread out very far apart. The central landmark was what made the desert an attractive place. The oasis at the center of the desert had special water not from the western sea and only the CIC knew the source of the water. If someone went through the desert to the oasis without drinking any water, he or she would see the Mirage Ruins and the galaxy within the training room at night. Drinking the water also healed all wounds and revealed the entrance to the CBA graveyard.

"Greeter," said a man's voice to my right.

We both jumped. The map rolled up and Uxor put it back in her desk. I looked to my right to see a male cherub wearing a dark blue robe with a single horizontal grey stripe at its center and grey edges on his sleeves. His wings were black and feathered. His feet were hidden beneath the cloud flooring. He was standing in front of a cloud portal I had not seen when I first entered the room. He may have been walking, but it appeared as if he was hovering towards us.

"Thank you for keeping Asanté Tekon Bulivard occupied during his wait," said he with his arms folded behind his back. I watched his neck turn toward me. "My name is Oberon," he said, "my apologies for the wait. Your patience is appreciated. I trust Greeter did an exceptional job of providing you an education during your wait?"

Greeter? Did he mean Uxor? I looked at Uxor with my eyes and kept my face aimed at Oberon. She took a sip from her glass and I felt as if her eyes met mine.

'Please, don't reveal me,' the soft, gentle voice echoed inside my head.

The voice. Her voice. It was Uxor. It was Uxor all along who I had been hearing from the very beginning. But, Uxor was a cherub. I thought only seraphim had the gift of telepathy? At least, I only saw four wings.

"I learned a lot," I said.

'Thank you, Tekon,' Uxor's voice echoed inside my head, 'one day I'll explain everything to you.'

I turned my head to her.

"Asanté Tekon Bulivard," said Oberon. He was standing by the cloud portal again and said, "come."

After the shocking revelation about the cherub or seraph, or whatever Uxor was, I at first did not hear what Oberon said, but my body knew and responded by following him through the cloud portal.

Chapter 12

I was in a cloud room. There were thirteen cloud pillars surrounding me in a circle. Each pillar was a different height and on each sat a cherub. Oberon sat on the pillar in front of me which was the shortest pillar. It was more like a stump, really. His feet were still hidden beneath the cloud flooring.

"Based off of your visual report we were able to determine exactly where the entrance you found to Greed's lair was," said Oberon. Was? "However," he continued, "by the time our team of chosens had arrived at the coordinates, the gateway had been moved."

"Now," said a female voice above me. She sounded like Uxor and I would have looked to see her had I not been previously instructed to only look at Oberon. "We have two questions we'd like to ask you. Will you please answer them?" Definitely Uxor.

"Yes, ma'am," I said.

"Did you find a way for a demon to sneak into CBA HQ?" asked a voice which undeniably belonged to the cherub who interrogated Vete and I before we received our missions. How was I supposed to answer? If the traitor angel was in the room, he would know I found out how the demons were coming and going, and even worse the CIC already wanted me to fail and would stop at nothing to make sure I did. What would happen if I said I did find the gateway?

"By answering that question," I said, "I'd alert the traitor angel if he is here to either change his entrance and exit route or that he is still safe."

"The apostate's voice as you described it is not a unique voice," said the deep voice belonging to one of the magistrate cherubim, "so it could be any angel with knowledge of heavenly artifacts, traps and pyrokinesis, which all seraphim have as well as many other an-gels, but none of us present have pyrokinesis."

"Yes, sir," I said, but how did I know none of the angels present were working with the traitor angel?

'Plead Refusal Clause 2,' echoed Uxor's voice.

What? What was Refusal Clause 2?

"So," said the interrogator, "did you find a way for a demon to sneak into CBA HQ?"

I did not know whether to trust Uxor or not, but with the way things had been going, she seemed more trustworthy than even Pro-fessor.

"I plead Refusal Clause 2," I said.

If looks could kill, I was sure Oberon's would have killed me.

Though I could not see his face, I could hear the anger and frustration when he asked, "how do you know about-?"

"Oberon," interrupted the deep voiced magistrate cherub, "he has pleaded Refusal Clause 2. We may no longer ask him any further questions."

"Besides," said the interrogator, "we now know that there is, indeed, a seraph aiding him. All the more reason to keep a close eye on him."

Oberon sighed and waved his hand at me. A cloud quickly grew from under me and completely engulfed me. Then it shrunk again and I was in my room in Babel Hotel.

Chapter 13

Electra was curled up on top of the bed. I plopped down next to her and she jumped. Her wide eyes stared at me for a moment as I laid on my back beside her. She walked in a circle on my torso, crouched down and slept. I thought about how I had not slept since I left to search for Reagan on my mission. I did not know how I just so happened to find Greed's lair. Greed had Reagan, or did I just imagine what I saw in the mirror? Either way, Greed knew where she was. I thought it would be a much longer process in finding out where she was, but I was right in thinking Greed had her or at least knew where she was. It was a greedy and later lustful feeling I felt emanating from the man who took her, and I felt the same feeling from the two police officers when they told me to quit or else I would never see her again.

Then there was Uxor to think about. I had heard her voice before I first awoke as a CBA. I had heard her voice often. Even during my hero nights in Anima Nex Vita there were times where her words gave me insight or her advice helped save me and the team. How did I not recognize her voice in person? Was it the lack of echo? Or was it because my mind was consumed with other things? Speaking of which, I needed to call Estelle and see what I owed her, but first a nice nap would be fine.

Before I set my hand down from petting Electra I looked at the back of my glove. Sure enough, there was a glowing white x, but Vadallat would have to wait. I carefully took my glove off and set it down beside me. I passed out. When I awoke, Electra was perched up on the kitchen counter pawing at the faucet over the kitchen sink. I sat up, took my coat off and sighed. My phone rang. The room number on the caller ID was Estelle's.

"Bonjour, Estelle," I said as I took off my other glove.

"Hello, Tekon. I figured you would be sleeping. How was your business?"

"It was, interesting. I learned a lot. Got some mysteries solved and some close to being solved, but I got a lot more questions now, too. How were the hero nights?" I hoped the conversation would end soon so I could get a much needed, much wanted, shower.

"They were amazing. Saving lives. People asked about you, you know. Especially Katniss." I could have sworn she winked when she said the name.

"Great. What'd you say?"

"Well, I told her you were on a business trip. Beatrice was with her when she asked and seemed a little upset."

I sighed. "Perfect."

"They are best friends, you know? Better not break Beatrice's heart, lover boy, or you will have no chance with Katniss."

"No. Estelle. Good Lord, no. Just, no."

"Oh Tekon, you do not have to lie to me. I can keep a secret. Anyway, I called to tell you that the angels have a special event for us tonight before the grand graduation ceremony tomorrow with the regular CB's, so we will have to postpone our ceremony."

"Oh, okay, thanks for letting me know, Estelle."

"It is my pleasure, Tekon. Be a good boy now."

"Yeah, right. Oh wait, what do I owe you?"

"I will let you now when you can repay me. For now, it is a favor you owe me."

"Oh good Lord. Alright. Just don't have me do anything stupid or crazy, alright?"

She chuckled and said, "we shall see."

She hung up. I sighed and put the phone down. It was time for a shower. After the shower I looked through the refrigerator for something to eat. There was a knock on the door and Electra jumped in the refrigerator.

"Dude, you, Electra, get out my fridge!" I said.

I left the door open and looked through the peephole. It was Vete. I told him to hold on and I got dressed. Electra eventually left the fridge and closed the door behind her. When I

227

let Vete in, I told him everything which happened since I last saw him up until I was brought back to my room.

"So let me get this straight," said Vete. He was sitting beside me at the minibar. Electra had snuck back onto the bed again to nap. Two of her tails were extended and wrapped around my waist. He continued, "a seraph has a crush on you-"

"She was a cherubim, actually."

"You know cherubim is plural, right?" he asked.

"What?"

"Singular is seraph and cherub. Plural is seraphim and cherubim or seraphs and cherubs."

"Oh, then what was Professor talkin' about when he-?"

"He meant that the Levis Tergum don't call multiple cherubs and seraphs cherubim and seraphim, which is the proper plural term. Instead they call them the plural of the singular term to imply that they all think and act the same and therefore have no individuality, and also because the cherubs and seraphs like proper and intellectual terms, so they get annoyed at being called cherubs and seraphs rather than cherubim and seraphim."

"So I've been saying the wrong thing this whole time? Well then. My bad. But anyway the cherub or seraph doesn't have a crush on me. I don't think angels have crushes, especially on humans."

"It wouldn't be the first time, and only seraphs are gifted with telepathy. They're also naturally gifted in pyrokinesis and telekinesis."

"How'd you find that out?"

"Vortex."

"Vortex?" I asked, "You've been to Vortex Castle? And I'm pretty sure Uxor is a cherub. I saw her and she only had four wings."

"Which is another thing. Natura Uxor is not a simple name. Angels only give their simple names to us, such as David or Professor or Greeter, but she introduced herself to you as Natura Uxor. That's not normal, and if that's her original angelic name, that's a sure sign she likes you. Also, she's obviously hiding the fact that she's a seraph from the CIC, which makes her a suspect for our case."

"Dude I don't think she's involved. Whatever she's involved in is probably different from our case. I mean even Greed wants her dead, and Greed's the one who's workin' with the traitor angel."

"Or maybe it's all an elaborate plan to get you to trust her until the moment she reveals her true colors. She's already gained your trust. She'll earn it again and again, until finally we realize it was her all along."

"Dude, she's been helping me from the beginning. She's checked in on me ever since I got here. Back when Anima's Next Heroes first started, without her voice in my head I would have died out there. If her goal was to kill me, or earn my trust and then betray me, she could've done it easily in those nights. Her voice sounded genuinely concerned about me during my mission and genuinely excited to meet me when she told me we were gonna meet."

"Listen. All I'm telling you is to be careful, Tekon. These are angels and demons we're dealing with, not your average thug back home or white collar thief. These beings think on a level much higher than ours, and their plans are much more elaborate than we can decipher."

"Yeah, I know. So what's Vortex like? How'd you get there? When'd you go?"

"I was put on trial again, as well, right after you, I think. With Angelic Speed I'm also able to talk fast, so the trial went by extremely quickly. When I was back in my room I went outside and heard some Citizen Souls talking about their cousin in Vortex City. I asked them about Vortex City and they told me where it was. They said that for us we'd have to fly through the storm and into the sea if we wanted to reach it. They said that flying over the storm was cheating and Vortex only reveals itself to us if we go through the storm. I took their word for it and it was no easy task. Even at my speed it was hard to fly through the storm and at one point I was forced to dive into the sea. Though the water wasn't clear blue, the dark blue water had such a strong current that even I couldn't swim straight, but the lower I was in the water, the weaker the currents were. Ironically, there was no current in the black water. So I tried to swim through it as fast as I could, but I had no visual and crashed into things a lot, so I slowed down. It wasn't long until I had to fight sea creatures, but I had help. I came across a group of CB's I hadn't seen before. There were two chosens and one regular. One chosen held back three humpback whales on his own. The other chosen was a girl who got swarmed by jellyfish. Five stung her, but she grabbed them by the stingers and flung them at a giant one."

"Dude."

"The regular used his sword as light for them to see," he continued, "his sword had a strong white glow. I didn't get a good view of any of them since I had my own battles to fight, but we made it to Vortex together. Vortex Castle on the outside is like a giant mirror. It reflects the sunlight from the sky to the surrounding water, making it friendly territory during the day. Vortex City is much the same, reflecting light as far as it can. The city looks like giant bubbles grouped together with a few towers here and there. I didn't go in the city, but the castle is all black marble on the inside with indescribable futuristic technology. The light sources are floating spheres of electric-blue light. The first thing I did was visit the archives."

"Oh wow. What'd you learn?"

"A lot. To start, the gates work as an entrance to virtually anywhere. While some are locked on to a certain location, such as the one you saw that led to Greed's lair, most are free standing. There are twelve gates and each gate has a time barrier on it in case someone wants to travel to another dimension."

"Wait, there are other dimensions we can travel to!?"

"We're in a different dimension right now, Tekon. Anyway, in the battle between Greed and that other chosen he talked about, the time barrier was broken. So that gateway is constantly over-adjusting itself and therefore traveling back and forth through time. You're blessed to have only lost a week, because the gate's time barrier also keeps its physical location in sync. If the gate over-adjusted by a millennium or even a century, when you left the lair you could have been in outer space due to the Earth and our solar system constantly moving."

"Okay I guess that makes sense. So if the gate was originally in my front yard, and the gate over-adjusted to 1972, it would go to the exact location where my yard was in 1972, but since the Earth is in 2012, the gate would be in outer space right? Or, if the gate traveled through time, but did not change physical location, the gate would still end up in outer space, but instead of the Earth being in front of it, Earth would be behind it, right?"

"That's correct. In your first example, the gate over-adjusted its physical location, whereas in your second example the gate over-adjusted its time location. But more importantly, Tekon, I found out what that book was in Hunter's room."

"What was it?"

"It was a book about the Holy Grail. I didn't get to read all the way through it before I was discovered, but-"

"Wait, discovered? What, were you not supposed to read that or something?"

"Well I sped past two guards to get there. Only certain people are allowed in the archives, but there was information I needed to find out and the CBA's who helped me to get to Vortex told me the archives had information on everything."

"So you dashed in and eventually got caught?"

"I didn't get caught. By the time the Levis Tergum realized I had gotten past them and switched their brains to fifth gear I was gone. But anyway the important thing is what I managed to find out about the Holy Grail. It grants one wish. Much similar to our rule-based wishes, but this wish has no rules. There are two possible ways to find it. One is through a designated gateway, the fifth gateway. It travels through time and space and only appears on Earth once a year. Only someone with extremely high spiritual potency will be taken to the Holy Grail through that gate."

"Okay so what's the other way?"

"Once every seven years, between the time when the lunar eclipses fall on the Feasts of The Temple and Passover, the Holy Grail will be in one location on Earth just up for the taking."

"Seriously!?"

"Yes. Then war breaks out. The demons who seek the grail to use the wish to end God and rule everything, against the angels who wish to defend the grail from demons. Yet neither side knows where the grail is."

"Except the demons will this time. They stole a girl who has the highest spiritual potency among CBA's."

"You're thinking they could use the girl to find the Grail by sensing it through the fifth gate? Or by finding it during the war?"

"Either way could be possible. They'll use her to search for the fifth gate until the lunar eclipse war. When is that, anyway?"

"April 15 to 29 of the year 2014."

"So a little less than two years … Do you think it could be Reagan?"

"If she became a CBA wouldn't she have awoken here?"

"They stole her, remember? Both physically and then spiritually when they snuck in here."

"That's possible. All the pieces could fit. And you saw her in Greed's lair, in the spiritual realm, so she may indeed be the girl."

"Then I'm gonna find her. I have less than two years to search and prepare for war. If I don't find her before then, I'm participating in that war and I'm saving her from Greed. If I have to, I'll find the Holy Grail myself and use the wish to wish for her freedom."

"That's great, Tekon, but-"

There was a knock on the door. Electra awoke and her tails squeezed me. Sagacious appeared at the door and opened it. Professor and David stood at the door.

'It was me who gave you the pants, Tekon,' echoed Uxor's voice in my head, 'They're special pants. They can hold a lot more things than they appear to.'

Were my pockets like a magic bag?

"Tekon?" asked David.

"Yes, sir?" I answered.

"You haven't heard a word I just said, have you?"

"No, sir. Sorry."

"Seraph talking to you?"

"That and my own wandering thoughts, yes, sir."

"Learn to multitask. Follow me and don't get lost."

"Yes, sir."

Funny he should tell me to learn to multitask. Back on Earth I could easily listen to two people at once and respond accordingly. I could even play two video-games at once, and had done so many times. We walked out the door and followed Professor and David down the spiral walkway.

"You named your pet Electra, correct?" asked David.

"Yes, sir."

"Well since you have yet to have your post-mission Prayer Life, you should do that now."

"Oh, yeah, forgot about that. Yes, sir. Will my body here still be walking, or ..?"

"It would be best if you had someone carry you."

"Well, Vete?"

Vete looked at me and said, "sure. Hop on."

Vete spread his wings and I piggy-backed onto him.

"Dear Lord our heavenly Father," I began.

Wait. How did David know I had not had my Prayer Life yet?

What I saw next was Reagan's face, except my vision was in black and white. Wind was blowing. I had something in my hands. It felt a little rough, but slightly smooth like paper. It was. I was carrying a stack of papers. I was

looking at a missing person flyer on a tele-
phone pole, the missing person being Reagan.
In my hand were more flyers. The bulge in the
front pocket of my jeans was probably a sta-
pler. Memories slowly came to my mind of the
events which had occurred since my last
Prayer Life and with them, without warning, the
flood of depression, misery, despair, hopeless-
ness, sadness, guilt and self-anger hit me like
a wrecking ball being slammed into a glass
tower. I fell to my knees in tears and shouted. I
slammed the side of my fist to the innocent
pole repeatedly as I shouted. The memories
finally ended, but the tears did not.

I looked at Reagan's face on the flyer
and shouted, "why, God!? Why!? Why did You
let this happen!? Why didn't anyone else do
anything!? Why did she get taken!? Why didn't
I get taken instead!? Why her!? Why did this
happen at all!?"

My mind fell to the thoughts of characters in the Bible, such as Joseph and Job.
Joseph, the dreamer, was given a dream by
God, and his life went in the complete opposite
direction of what his dream showed him. The
second youngest son was given a dream in
which all his family bowed to him, but then he
was thrown into slavery, and later into prison.
Job lost everything. In both of those situations,
what the enemy intended for evil, God turned it
around for good. Joseph became second in
command of all of Egypt, saved the country

and a future nation. Job was given back every-thing he had lost and more. My mind was brought to Romans 8:28 KJV which says: And we know that all things work together for good to them that love God, to them who are the called according to his purpose. I cried all the more.

"God," I said through my tears, "I know I'm supposed to trust in You, and I know you've turned things around for others, Lord. Please turn things around for me. Please bring Rea-gan back."

I slowly stood back up. The last memory which flowed into me showed me I was not the only one setting up flyers. The youth group as well as the college and career group from my church were also setting up flyers throughout the Kansas City area. There were churches in other cities setting up flyers as well. I also had been deeply depressed over the days. I still had not faced Reagan's parents. I lost all moti-vation for school, though I still trudged through the work. My grades were slipping, but were still good enough. I was still involved in church. Being at church was one of the hardest things, being in the same space as her parents, but it was also relieving being able to feel God's presence strongly during worship. At home, if I was not doing schoolwork or driving through the city hoping to spot Reagan on the streets, I was sleeping the days away, trying to escape the depression and live in my dreams. In my dreams, Reagan was alive. In my dreams, I saved her. Unfortunately, dreams must end. The world kept spinning. Reality laughed, mocked me, telling me to wake up, get up, and live life.

Something in my other front pocket vibrated. I pulled out my slim black smartphone to see a text from Anna. She had been sending me encouraging texts about finding Reagan at random times. This text was different.

It read, "Hey. Hope you're doing alright. Once you're done we should meet up for some fro-yo! It's hot!" There was an emoticon of a sweaty smiley face at the end.

"Sure," I texted back.

I looked around and remembered I had a partner with me as well on this route. I hoped he did not hear my crying and screaming earlier. What was his name, again? Blake, or was it Jet? No. Wait. His name was Blake, but as a kid people called him Jet because he liked airplanes. Jet was a tall, muscular guy with black hair and brown eyes. Now where was he?

"Hey Asanté," said a distant voice. I looked to see Blake walking towards me. He wore blue jeans and a black tee-shirt. His hair went just above his ears and he wore a black, neatly trimmed beard.

"Hey," I said.

"You ready to go? Looks like we had a lot of extras."

"Oh."

"Yeah. I already finished the route, so we can just save those for next time," he said, referencing the stack of flyers in my hand.

"Yeah. Anna invited me to hang out and eat some froyo. Wanna come?"

"Yeah. I got the text, too, from Rachel. Sure, I'm up for that. You alright, man?"

"I'm living."

"Yeah. One day at a time."

We walked a few blocks to a green SUV. I noticed I had keys in my pocket as well. We got in the vehicle and I turned the key. The radio came on and there was a pastor speaking.

"Let's begin this sermon with a prayer," he said, "dear Lord our heavenly Father ..."

I was standing among other chosens. Someone, I thought it was David, was giving a speech somewhere up front.

"So enjoy your last night of chosen initiation," he said, "because as of now your training is complete. You are full fledged chosen. Tomorrow, after the grand graduation ceremony with the rest of your fellow Class B Angels, you will be given new rooms in the central plane and join your fellow graduates in armor remodification. I think some of you are tired of wearing itchy medieval armor." The crowd chuckled and so did I, thinking of Terminator and Larry. I wondered how they had been. David continued, "you will all get to choose-"

'Oh, you're back,' echoed Uxor's voice in my head, 'thank you for not revealing me to the

240

CIC. If you will meet me in the morning on top of Babel Hotel at sunrise, I will begin to explain everything to you so that you may trust me. I want to help you find the traitor angel.'

The chosens cheered and screamed. People were jumping, hugging, flying and high-fiving. Something exploded in the sky. I looked to see fireworks of red, blue, green, yellow and various other colors explode with magnificence. We had done it. We had graduated. Funny thing was I was to graduate from high school on Earth the next day. It felt good to see everyone happy and cheery. Vete appeared in front of me with two glasses of water. He handed one to me. I then realized where we were. We were in the eastern desert. Based off of Vete giving me water to drink, we were at the oasis.

"To new adventures," he said with a smile.

"To saving the world, eternity, and finding Reagan," I said.

We clinked glasses and drank. To him it must have been like watching something getting swallowed into nothingness. After my first swallow the scenery changed dramatically. An old Romanian style colosseum built itself all around us from the sand. Beyond the broken walls I could see what appeared to be a castle as well. The night sky was no longer barren, but now filled with lights and wonder as the stars and galaxies were crystal clear. I handed Vete the glass back and he disappeared.

'Beautiful, isn't it?' echoed Uxor's voice.

Vete reappeared and we sat at the top of a support pillar. The sky was indescribably beautiful. It was as if NASA took the most beautiful photo shots from space and submitted them to the angels to make a hundred times better.

"You know," I said, "you never explained to me how Uxor telling me her real name meant that she had a crush on me."

"Has," he said, "and that's because their natural names are only spoken among God and the angels. The only times angels gave their real names to humans was when they showed a love interest beyond the blanket love for all humanity which has dwindled down over the eons."

"Eons? Earth's only a few thousand years old dude."

"Our Earth."

"Vete, this isn't heaven. Even here you shouldn't believe everything you read."

"What I read was true, Tekon. It's like I tried to tell you earlier, the angels ha-"

"Well hello, Tekon," interrupted Estelle from above. She was laying on the ledge of a part of the colosseum just above us with her head sticking out. "I found you," she said. She flew down to us and stood on air in front of us.

"Bonjour, Estelle," I said.

"Hey," said Vete.

"Hello, Vete," she said unenthusiastical-ly.

"Still upset?" he asked.

"You hit me on the head," she said.

"It was an accident," he said.

"Want to say it again three times?" she asked.

"I've said it a billion times," he said, "I'm sorry! It was an accident."

"I've seen you use Angelic Speed and weave through a crowd of people without touching a single hair. Admit it. You are just jealous I scored higher than you on the critical combat exam and so you decided to take it out on me by hitting me in the back of the head!"

"We both know I should have scored higher. Your fighting was weak, your tech-niques were sloppy and your form was hideous, but I did NOT hit you on the back of your head!"

I face-palmed. "Guys," I said, but was ignored.

"Say it one more time so I can see you humiliate yourself," she said.

"You still think I'm lying!?" he asked.

"Guys," I said a little louder.

"Did you see yourself!?" she asked, "you looked like a dying duck!"

"And you looked liked a chicken with its head cut off!" he retaliated.

"GUYS!" I shouted. Estelle gasped and looked at me. "Y'all need to solve your problems without insults and shouting," I said.

"Sorry, Tekon," she said, "so sorry."

"Now Estelle, what were you looking for me for?"

"I just wanted to tell you that since there is still time, the rest of the group wanted to fight tonight at midnight, but it is up to you since you are our leader."

"Yeah, I'm up for it. Great way to end the night."

Perhaps Uxor would help out, too, like she had before.

Estelle smiled and said, "alright. I will let everyone know, unless you want to tell Katniss yourself?" She winked.

I face-palmed again. "Good Lord, Estelle. No. Just, go. Go tell everyone."

She chuckled and said, "alright, Tekon. I will go, and I will be sure to allow you plenty of times to be a hero in front of Katniss and save the damsel in distress." She winked again.

"Estelle!"

She laughed and said, "Oh Tekon, you are too fun." She gave one last smile and flew away.

"Dude," I said to Vete, "I think she likes you."

"Is Uxor's voice messing with your head?" If it was not Vete I was talking to, I would think the question was a joke.

"Dude I'm serious. It's like the movies. You start off hating each other and fighting a lot. Then as time goes on y'all grow closer and become friends, but still feisty. Then by the end of the TV series or movie or movie series or whatever, y'all love each other."

"Either Uxor's messing with your head or you're just crazy."

"Dude I'm serious. I've seen it in the movies and TV series and everything. It's so classic I'm pretty sure it's Shakespeare."

"As classic as a half angel, half human player?"

"What?" I asked.

"Well if we're gonna talk about my love-life, let's talk about yours."

"Dude, I ain't got one right now."

"You must be layered. You are lying through your teeth."

"What are you talkin' about?"

"First, it was Hope. Then there's rumors about you and Katniss having a special night in Anima Nex Vita. They're calling it Anima Las Vegas."

"Dude! What are you talking about!? That night was a complete misunderstanding!"

"Then there's Uxor, or Greeter as she's known to the rest of us, who's been speaking soft words into your head since you first awoke as a CBA."

"And do you see me with any of them right now!?"

"And then there's Gabriella from Anima Nex Vita."

"Hey man I didn't say I like her. She's fine, but I didn't say I like her."

"You didn't say you didn't either."

"But you do."

"I don't think a half-angel and a Citizen Soul would go well together."

"Still no denial. At least you don't lie to me."

"Don't change the subject. You know what I've learned about you, Tekon?"

"What, Vete?"

"You like the mystery. Hope doesn't speak, Uxor's face can't be seen, Katniss keeps to herself and hides things, and Gabriella seems to appear and disappear out of your night life like she's Sagacious. And you want to unravel all of those mysteries."

"Wow. That's ... Wow. Well. I don't know what to say, except, ... That'll make a great story for a book one day."

Chapter 14

After a while of stargazing, the chosens began to return to Babel Hotel to eat and celebrate. I was going to eat with Anima's Next Heroes at our favorite restaurant, but first I wanted to get Electra a treat. I took her out of my room and began to walk down the spiral walkway with her. Electra looked everywhere except for where she was going as we walked. I took her to a pet store in the shopping section. It was a grey building with a picture of a dog on one window and a cat on another window. There were big yellow letters above the entrance which read "Bob's Pet Store."

The store looked much bigger from the inside, though the layout was plain. There was a simple white ceiling, white tile flooring and countless rows of shelves. To my right was a clerk behind a counter with a cash register who did not look happy to see me. He was a big, older, tan man with grey hair and grey chest hair sticking out of his yellow polo shirt.

"You know only the restaurant section gives free things to you people, don'tcha?"

You people?

"Oh, yes, sir. I have money," I said as I remembered the money Terminator had given me. It was still in my pocket though it had been washed many times.

"Hmph. An Outsider hirer ya, or did you rob someone?"

Outsider?

"Sir?"

"Ah forget it. Just hurry up and buy something."

"Yes, sir."

What was his problem? Outsiders? Was he referring to the local souls who lived outside of Babel Hotel? You people? Was he referring to angels and CB's? I was looking at a chew toy in an aisle and took my eyes off of Electra for one second. Big mistake.

"Hey hey hey!" I heard the man yell from a distance. I looked to see Electra sitting at a cross section gnawing on a shiny rubber fish she held between her two front paws. Wrapped in each of her nine tails were other toys. "Control your animal!" yelled the man.

"Yes, sir. Sorry, sir," I said.

"Yeesh," he said. I heard him walk away while mumbling under his breath.

"Electra!" She stopped gnawing on the toy as her eyes rose to me. "Put the toys back," I said firmly. Her tails extended in different directions as she walked towards me with the toy in her mouth and dropped it at my feet. "Good girl. We'll get one toy."

"Just ONE!?" shouted a high pitched voice which filled the air.

Electra jumped onto my chest with so much force she knocked me down. Her tails

248

quickly retracted, wrapped around me and squeezed.

"Awe, did I scare da poor wittle kitty?" asked the voice, followed by hysterical laughter.

The lights flickered and Electra shuddered. I slowly got up.

"What do you want with me now?" I shouted, "and why did you save me back there?" I started walking out of the aisle.

"One question at a time, boy. It's not what III want with you."

There was a thud in the distance, followed by another and another which kept getting louder and sounding closer. I looked to my left to see the shelves falling like dominoes. The shelf closest to me began to fall and I jumped out of the aisle, but as I was in midair something slammed me towards the ground. I landed in a pushup stance to not crush Electra. In front of me was the back of a pair of white high-top sneakers with a bright red x on the heels.

"It's what HE wants with you!" said the voice, followed by hysterical laughter.

X-kneot slowly walked away from me, allowing me to get up. He turned around and God's Wrath materialized in his left hand.

"Jesus wept," I said. Lord's Tear appeared in my right hand.

"Alright boys," said the voice, "I want a dirty fight! No holds barred! All kicks to the groin!" Then in a much deeper, booming voice he said, "FIGHT!"

X-kneot rushed me, but blocking him was simple. He hopped back.

"You know it's not smart fighting me here," I said, "with all the chosens and angels around."

In less than a few seconds he flew to me, I heard him say, "shut up," felt a sharp pain on my right side, then pain in my left shoulder and the left side of my face, followed by my back. I fell to the ground, probably from a brick wall, and landed on my knees. Anima Nex Vita's unforgettable night cry filled my ears. In one hit, X-kneot had knocked me out of an underground store into an aboveground wall of a building. Since when did he get so strong? My body ached all over and my head ached tremendously, but I slowly got up and looked at Electra. She seemed to be alright physically.

"Electra," I said, "time to fight."

"Indeed," said X-kneot behind me.

There was a sharp pain in my kidneys and I was sent flying through the revolving door of Babel Hotel to the wall on the other side. I slammed into the wall with Lord's Tear stabbed into it. The central pole of the revolving door was snapped in half and fell. The glass shattered. X-kneot was just beyond the rubble. He held out his open palm in my direction and the rubble flew towards me. I quickly twisted Lord's Tear and pulled it out. Wind pushed me towards the flying shards of glass, but I dodged them somehow. Next were the broken revolving door panels. The wind pushed me through the hole in one and a part of the pole flew inches under my face. Then I saw the top of X-kneot's hood pass under me. I landed gently on the ground and turned around just in time to block God's Wrath. Locked in stalemate, I tried to hit him with my big wings, but they were blocked by his.

"Electra!" I yelled, "electrify!"

Electra looked at X-kneot and opened her mouth, but X-kneot quickly flew up. X-kneot's sudden takeoff hooked our swords and pulled me up as Electra shot electricity from her mouth. Before I knew it, I was high above Babel Hotel and there was a black line down its center from where Electra had shot it. The table on top of the rooftop was also shot through. It split in half and each half fell. I knew what was coming next. I unhooked Lord's Tear from God's Wrath and flew as fast as I could towards the rooftop. X-kneot tried to pursue me, but a rocket whizzed by him. Wearing a white coat in the black sky made him an easy target for the local souls. For once I was glad the criminals were out. As I approached the rooftop I heard Zenith roar. The clouds above Babel Hotel began to swirl and I knew a tornado was coming. Zenith was going to destroy Babel Hotel and all the chosens inside. Was X-kneot's plan to destroy me in there as well? What

251

about his escape route? The gate would be closed off unless there was another some-where.

Chosens flocked out of Babel Hotel like small birds taking off when a dog runs to them. Most flew to the forest, but some, including all of Anima's Next Heroes, flew to meet me at the top of the Hotel. When I landed, Vete and Sagacious appeared in front of me.

Vete looked up and said, "Sagacious, you know what to do."

Sagacious nodded his head and went to meet the other chosens.

"Listen up," yelled Sagacious over the wind, "this is how we're going to do this!"

I almost did a double take. I had forgot-ten simian guises could speak.

"I'm guessing that blast of lightning that sliced the hotel in half was Electra," said Vete.

"Yeah, it was an accident," I said.

"Well now's her chance to fix it," he said, "Sagacious is going to lead chosens with wind-based battle prayers to protect Babel Hotel from that tornado that's forming, but that'll do no good if the hotel ends up like that table there. Electra needs to wrap her tails around the building."

"Tekon!" I turned around to see Estelle run to me. "What is going on!?" she asked.

The hotel creaked.

"Alright let's do this now!" shouted Sagacious.

He stood with a foot on either side of where the hotel split and some chosens flew in a circle around him in the opposite direction of the funnel cloud quickly dropping. They shouted various things and a tornado of their own began to form which spun in the opposite direction of the oncoming tornado. Zenith roared in the distance.

"Electra!" I shouted over the wind, "I need you to wrap your tails around the building, now!"

She only looked at me with intense fear in her eyes. Estelle grabbed my arm.

"Tekon, we can stop the hotel from falling apart," she said, "just give the word."

"Have Kalel and Kakkarot use their strength prayers and each take a side and keep the hotel from falling as best they can," I said, "when they do that, Katniss needs to use her multiplication prayer so that we can have as many clones as possible."

"But Tekon," she said, "Katniss can't-"

Thunder boomed. The building shook. My first thought was on Electra, but her lightning was silent compared to what I heard. Thunder boomed again. My heart raced. Anima Nex Vita only had a storm on one night of the year. The Night of Chaotic Cleansing. Vete's face grew dim, and so did Estelle's.

"Forget the plan," said Vete, "we need to get any remaining chosens out of here."

"What about the people!?" asked Estelle.

"The people will be fine," I said, "for them this is the one night they can't die, but for us, we most certainly will die if we stay."

She nodded her head and said, "alright."

"Anima's Next Heroes," I said, "help the other chosens escape."

"Yes, sir," she said and flew off.

On the Night of Chaotic Cleansing, first a piece of the hurricane from the western sea would branch off and head to Anima Nex Vita, bringing a thunderstorm, followed by razor sharp hail and then tornados. Then a sandstorm from the eastern desert would blow in, followed by an earthquake which stretched to the western sea and northern mountains. The earthquake would cause the northern volcanos to erupt and send lava down to the city. When the tornados began to suck up lava they became lava tornados. The earthquake also caused a tsunami from the western sea to crash into the city, which created whirlpools once the water was sucked up by the tornados. The hail, lightning strikes, tornados, lava flow and earthquakes did not end. Also, all plants and animals in Anima Nex Vita, minus those summoned by the use of a second wish, became carnivorous and toxic to the touch. The storm clouds trapped the ash from the volcanos and lava and created sulfuric air in the city. The end phases were signaled by a giant red lightning strike on the water. A blizzard would blow in from the west, bringing the temperature under the sulfuric clouds to absolute zero. Everything besides the different types of tornados, the lightning strikes, earthquake, sandstorm and hailstorm would be flash frozen, but people would still be conscious and feel every bit of the pain. Then the temperature below the sulfuric clouds would jump to Planck Temperature and the air literally exploded. The sulfur in the air ignited, causing the explosion and preventing anyone from seeing the highly radioactive meteor plummet towards the city. Once it crashed into the city and was struck by red lightning, a black hole was created.

The beginning phases could kill the angelic half of a CBA. Once the earthquake hit, the CBA could die completely. Full angels could also die, but they were reborn immediately after the cleansing. The black hole could completely erase a soul from existence. It was said only God could survive the final black hole; angels would not be reborn.

'TEKON!' Uxor's voice boomed in my head, giving me a headache.

I put my hands to me head and fell to my knees. Vete had already disappeared. I started coughing.

'Tekon!' came Uxor's voice again, 'you have to get out of the city!'

I saw Sagacious disappear and the other chosens flew to the forest. Zenith roared and a blast of wind stung my face and blew me off of the rooftop. I could not escape the powerful wind current. I looked ahead of me and saw a helicopter on a collision course with me, or me with it.

I yelled, "Mutatio machina!" and clapped my hands together.

The helicopter bent at unusual angles and began to look almost humanoid with the large propeller over its head and the two machine guns on its arms. The helicopter robot flipped over me in midair while firing off in the distance, but I could tell the robot was not shooting aimlessly. It was shooting at Zenith. Once the helicopter robot passed me, I heard Zenith roar again. I flew towards Zenith and the helicopter robot transformed back into a helicopter and fell. Zenith roared again and another powerful gust of wind flung me towards the ground. Hail began to fall. Another roar. I looked around me to see cars being lifted in the air and flung towards me as I fell, unable to recover. I yelled the prayer again.

The two closest cars transformed into humanoids and hugged me as I fell. They shielded me from the other cars. When we hit the ground I only saw black. Then the car robots moved and I could see light as they sucked back in their airbags.

"Thanks," I said to one.

It nodded its head and gave me a thumbs up, but then its head disappeared.

There was a clunk on the ground a few feet away. It was its head. The body of the robot fell in front of me and there stood X-kneot. He stood as if the hail had no affect on him, as if he were wearing a cloak of wind which protected him from the elements. The other car robot ran to him, but X-kneot impaled it. I watched the robot fall in front of me. Then he swung down God's Wrath upon me. I jumped back and tripped over car rubble, which saved me from an air slash. I landed on my back with my wings propping me up. X-kneot rushed me, but I kicked God's Wrath out of his hands. He tried to jump on me, aiming for his feet to land on my face, but a white-robed figure palmed him in his side and sent him flying. Vete extended his hand to me.

'Tekon you can't fight him here! You need to leave, now!' Uxor's voice boomed in my head.

I took Vete's hand and he helped me up.

"My shield protects me from the hail," he said, "you know your best bet to get rid of him is to keep him here and then leave at the last second when it's too late for him."

"Can you do that?" I asked.

"If I can't, you can," he said, "calmly turn around."

I turned around and saw X-kneot striking at Vete's invisible barrier.

"So where's Zenith?" I asked.

"Sagacious has already found Zenith," said Vete.

"Where is he?" I asked.

"Don't ignore me!" screamed X-kneot.

He sent a gust of wind at us, but we did not feel the slightest breeze. Vete grabbed my shoulder and the next thing I saw was a suburb. Sagacious stood in front of us and walked under Vete's protection. Zenith's roar boomed in my ears. I could hear the flapping of its wings. Sagacious pointed at a house and Zenith was perched on top. Though invisible, I could tell where the dragon was because of the hail falling on its wind armor. Lightning struck a nearby house and a tornado began to howl behind us.

"Pretty soon visibility will be slim," said Vete. He was right. Around us, the dark neighborhood became orange and blue as sand raged and hail fell. "I can't use Angelic Speed or Angel Dance without seeing where I'm going," yelled Vete over the storm, "I could run us into a wall."

"So I need to use my power then," I yelled, "but if I don't take out X-kneot I don't think he'll let us leave."

I summoned Lord's Tear and was about to stab the ground, but stopped when I saw a flash of white out of the corner of my eye. Of course, it could have been the tip of either Vete's or Sagacious' wings, so I proceeded to stab the ground, twist and pull up. A whole in the ground began to open up, but was quickly closed. X-kneot. He stood a few feet in front of us, sword drawn. I just then realized he always held his sword in his left hand, which mirrored my right hand. He knelt down and slapped the ground with his other hand. A burst of wind blew in all directions from where he smacked the ground and grew into a dome around us. There was no longer any falling hail or raging sand nearby.

"Okay," I said, "so maybe he could still escape at the last second."

The ground began to shake. Earth-quake. Zenith roared loudly as the dragon flapped its wings and I felt the ground lift. I watched other houses shrink and realized what Zenith was doing. We now had a floating plat-form above the earthquake to fight on. I pulled Electra off of my chest and set her down, but two of her tails refused to let go of my legs.

"Stay," I told her.

She looked at me and I unwrapped her tails.

"You plan on taking him alone?" asked Vete.

"Seems like the movie thing to do," I said, "he's my responsibility, after all."

"That doesn't mean you have to face him alone," said Vete, "there's no reason I can't take him out for you."

"True, but this is between me and him, or, my other me," I said, "one of those things you have to take care of on your own. Your arch nemesis type thing, the one and only enemy for you, something like that."

"So your arch nemesis is yourself?"

"It seems so."

I rushed out to X-kneot with a slash. He deflected to his right with God's Wrath, grabbed my right arm with his right hand and sent a left knee towards my kidneys. My small right wing blocked his knee and my large right wing struck him in his chest, sending him back and releasing my arm. I stepped towards him and came down with a slanted slash again, but he crouched down below it and kicked both of my shins simultaneously, causing my to fall. As I fell he brought both of his knees up towards my face. I brought my free hand to meet his knees, launched myself up and backflipped away in the air. X-kneot jumped up and rushed me with a slash, but I dodged to the right and sent a left kick towards his stomach. He blocked with his right small wing and it wrapped around my leg as he tossed God's Wrath in the sky. Then he walked up my sternum with a series of quick knuckle punches, spun vertically and tossed me up in the air to be struck as God's Wrath came down.

I landed on my back on X-kneot's knee with him to my right. He sent a left elbow towards my sternum, but I palmed his face with my left hand. He blew a gust of wind at me to push me away, but I hooked Lord's Tear to the back of his neck and used the momentum of being blown away to help pull his chest into my left knee. I then spun around behind him, wrapped my legs around his waist, pulled him over me and slammed him into the ground behind me. I rolled forward and barely dodged a heel kick. I got up and turned around in time to block God's Wrath. X-kneot tried to headbutt me, but I jumped back and instead sent a right front kick towards his face. He instead grabbed my leg with his right hand, pulled me towards him and sent a left kick towards my head which I blocked with my right large wing. I jumped and sent a left roundhouse kick towards his face, but he blocked with his right large wing. Still holding my leg, he spun around and slammed me to the ground. I rolled over and he was going to impale me with God's Wrath, but just as the blade was inches from my face a furry white hand palmed X-kneot in the face which knocked him a few feet away. X-kneot let out a growl and came to slash at Sagacious, but Sagacious deflected it and slapped X-kneot in the face. Then he helped me up as X-kneot was staggering and disappeared.

"That simian guise was Vete's, no doubt," said X-kneot.

From the edge of the platform I could see flames.

"The lava has entered the city!" shouted Vete, "and the tsunami has probably hit the west side by now!"

"Then I'll just have to wrap this up quickly!" said X-kneot.

He slashed the air, sending an unavoidable gust of wind at me. It stung my face and sent me hurtling into the air. I recovered and deflected God's Wrath before it impaled me. X-kneot blew a gust of wind at me which slammed me into the wall of the dome of air, or so I thought, but it felt more solid than air. Zenith roared in my ear and I was smacked down to the ground. I landed on my back and X-kneot was immediately on top of me. He held an open palm above me and I could feel wind being sucked out of me. I tried to close my mouth, but I hardly had any air in my lungs to begin with.

I think Sagacious tried to hit him because he swung God's Wrath around and a blast of wind made something crack the ground. He had all of my wings pinned by his and covered my arms as well. I thought I heard Vete yell my name, but I could not tell for sure. I definitely heard Zenith roar. My throat tightened and my vision began to blur.

I could not think of anything, but screamed for Jesus in my head. I heard two booms like thunder and saw a flash of red. The vacuum stopped. I gasped for air, rolled over and coughed as X-kneot fell beside me. There was a loud thud as Zenith, now visible, fell behind him. The grey dragon with mirror-like scales had a large round torso and a long

262

neck. With Zenith unconscious, the air dome ceased to exist and the ground around us began to fall into the earthquake and lava below.

I remained in the air and Vete appeared by my side. His shield protected us from the harmful elements. Sagacious was hung over his shoulders and Electra, who was cradled in his other arm, quickly latched onto my waist like a belt. I petted her and looked at Sagacious.

"Is he gonna be okay?" I asked.

"They heal quickly," said Vete.

"What happened?"

"They got struck by red lightning."

"Red lightning!? We don't have much time!"

I looked down to see if X-kneot and Zenith were still down below, but I could not see them anywhere among the chaos.

"In Jesus' name, amen," I said softly.

I released Lord's Tear and we flew up above the clouds while Sagacious awoke. Above the dark clouds was a starry sky. One star in particular was very bright. There was also a full lunar eclipse, but neither of those new sights surprised me. It was Natura Uxor, or Greeter, who caught my attention. She hovered in front of us and held a bamboo sword in her hand. Vete said she was a seraph, but I still only saw four wings.

"I'm glad you're alright, Tekon," said Uxor.

"Vete," I began, "this is-"

"A fallen seraph," he finished.

Uxor remained silent.

"Dude, we've gone over this. She's-"

"Only seraphs can communicate tele-pathically. Also, only seraphs have ever shown romantic feelings for humans."

"Uxor, sorry about this. Vete and I need to talk-"

"There's nothing you can say to change the truth, Tekon," said Vete, "I had my suspicions from when you first told me your story, but seeing her now confirms it. Back in Vortex when I read up on the history of the angels I came across a story about her. It said that she coveted the love of humans and sought out that love for herself. When she found a human to her liking, they began to fall in love. When this was found out she was banished as a seraph, but the banishment was kept silent because only Lucifer and his angels had fallen, and the seraphs wanted to keep up appearances as the most holy angels. So to save face they clipped her bottom wings and introduced her as a new cherub."

Natura Uxor remained silent.

"That's far out there, Vete," I said.

"Vortex records don't lie," said Vete, "the archives contain many hidden truths that the higher up angels don't want public."

"Then why would they keep records in a place where people can get to it!?" I asked, "that doesn't make any sense. How do you know the stories aren't lies?"

"He's not lying, Tekon," said Uxor in a sad tone. I looked at her. "Back then my name was Regis Filia," she said. I saw a single, small, shining tear fall from where her face would have been. "I did not originally seek human affection," she said.

"No," said Vete, "originally God gave you an angelic lover after He discussed with you His plans for making Earth. You were to help guide humans on a path of love."

"Who was your lover?" I asked.

Her long hair shook in response to her shaking her head.

Vete began, "her lover was-"

"No!" she screamed, "don't say it!"

"Awe why not!?" boomed a loud high pitched voice. The voice. "I'm as interested as ever to find out who the secret lover of Regis Filia was!" it said.

"You've GOT to be kidding me!" I said in frustration.

We all turned our heads in every direction, trying to find the source of the voice.

"I was told Regis Filia chose to worship the Lord in the holiest corner of heaven for all eternity in a room that only He enters. Clever lie," said the voice.

"Why are you still here?" asked Vete.

"I'm here to see all the fun!" answered the voice with glee.

265

"Not you," said Vete, "you."

He was talking to Regis Filia, or Natura Uxor, or Greeter.

"I wanted to make sure Tekon was well," she responded.

"You must be layered!" said the voice, "I think we all know there is more to it than that, deary! That star will come crashing down any time now and instead of getting the runts to safety you're here chatting it up!"

"You want to die," said Vete.

Even the voice remained silent then. I stared at Uxor, but she still said nothing.

"Is it true?" asked Sagacious.

The dark clouds were white now, but not from a nature of peace. I could feel the temperature quickly rising from the oncoming meteor.

"WELL IS IT!?" boomed the voice.

'You need to go now, Tekon,' her soft, gentle voice echoed inside my head, 'not even Vete's faith will protect you from the meteor and dark hole. The King of Kings has set it that way.'

"We have to go, Vete," I began to say.

'To Vortex Castle.'

"To Vortex Castle," I echoed.

"She told you that, didn't she?" asked Vete.

I looked at him.

"Did I just miss a telepathic conversation?" asked the voice.

"It's time to go," said Vete. It was certainly time to go. The meteor was only seconds away from plummeting into Anima Nex Vita. Vete tried to speed us away as fast as he could pulling Sagacious, Electra and I, but his spiritual potency must have been low from the constant use of his shield and Angelic Speed in the past few minutes. We were flying fast, but not fast enough.

'Don't look back,' Uxor's voice echoed softly inside my head.

Don't look back. Remember Lot's wife, but I looked back anyway. As if in slow motion, the giant, black, burning meteor fell on top of Uxor and pushed her down through the clouds. There was a flash of blinding light and then total darkness and total silence immediately after.

Chapter 15

To a friend: I'm still counting down the days.

Though I did not know how long it would be until I found Reagan, counting down felt more hopeful than counting up. Counting up, I did not know when I would see her again, but counting down gave me the feeling of hope, because eventually the number would reach zero. In order for the timer to reach zero, I could not be dead. My soul could not be erased. I had to live. I had to survive to find her. I could not ever give up. I could not ever forget.

I heard slurred words. Something about a list. Survival. I opened my eyes. I was laying on a bed in a black room with small light blue spheres floating around. They must have been the light source for the room. There was a black door at the end of the room I was facing when I sat up. I was struck with a massive headache and ringing in my ears. There must have been a window, because in a rectangle I saw David. He was talking to someone.

"I don't know how I could have missed her on the list!" He sounded very frustrated.

"I've never heard of an angel that want-ed to die," said a familiar voice. It was much closer and came from my right. Vete was laying in a bed beside mine. He stared at the blue spheres. "And when they die," he continued, "are they reborn the same as they were when they died? Or when they were first created? Do they retain their memories?"

The black door opened and the space around the foot of my bed was filled with three figures in black hoods with a white x across their chest.

"Yo, Tekon! You're black, yo!"

"Quiet down, man. Hey, are you okay?"

The two male voices sounded familiar to me.

"Who are you?" I asked.

They each pulled their hoods down to reveal themselves as Hope, Terminator who was wearing black shades, and Larry who did not have a biker helmet or wooden shield at his side. Hope sat on my bed beside me.

"Oh hey guys," I said as I rubbed my eyes and placed my hand to my head, "how do you know I'm black?"

Hope smiled.

"Yo 'cause you're shirtless, yo!" said Terminator.

"I said quiet down, man," said Larry.

I looked down and saw I was, indeed, topless.

"Whoa!" I said and immediately reached down to my left, assuming my coat was there.

I grabbed something and flung it to my chest. Hope smiled even wider as if to silently chuckle.

"What's that?" asked Terminator.

I looked down to see Electra looking up at me.

"This is Electra," I said, "she's a furry dragon. A creature obviously not found on Earth."

Hope stretched out her hand and Electra licked it. Hope smiled and began to pet her as a tail wrapped around her arm.

"Hey, Vete," said Larry.

"Hi guys," said Vete.

"Who's the babe holding your coat?" Larry asked me.

All eyes followed the direction of his stare.

Sitting on the bed to the left of mine was a girl with long black hair which went past her waist. She wore an icy blue short-sleeve gown with long snow-white gloves which went a little past her elbows. She had two long snow-white feathered wings which were gracefully folded behind her back. She sat, her back upright and poised, with one hand over the other placed on top of my folded coat. Her mysterious hazel eyes starred into mine. She smiled and opened her mouth to say something, but was cut off by David who, pen and clipboard in hand, stormed in.

"I don't know how I could have missed you on the list!" he said in frustration, "I am VERY thorough about my list! I've not once missed someone who became a CB!"

A girl David missed on his list? Was she the girl who was stolen? If so, then I was farther away from Reagan than I thought, but if she was the girl with the highest spiritual potency, then perhaps I could get her to help me find the Grail.

Professor walked in.

"Oh come now. Don't feel bad about it. Everyone makes mistakes now and then," said Professor.

"Bah," David huffed. He folded his arms, then unfolded them and said, "you three must be blessed and highly favored to have survived the NCC." He then clicked his pen and prepared to write. "So just, who are you?" he asked in annoyance.

She began to open her mouth again, but Professor spoke.

"Oh come now, David. Be a little more polite," said Professor, "miss, would you please tell us your name?" Her eyes searched everyone in the room and finally fell on mine.

'You know exactly who I am.'